LEAK

REVIVAL OF THE REALM

By L Bailey Bastian

ISBN: 978-0-578-43823-8
ISBN-13: 978-0-578-43823-8

DEDICATION

This volume is dedicated to my siblings, Kenneth Bailey, Barbara Bailey, Gladys Ross and the late Margaret Moore.

CHAPTERS

CHAPTER ONE

Frank knew it would be near impossible to outrun his incredibly fast twenty-one-year-old daughter, Lacey, which is why he chased after her in his sedan. He was in good health, but at sixty, he was much slower than he was in his youth. Maybe it was the rod in his hip from an old college football injury that left him with a permanent limp. Regardless of a bum leg, he would not have been able to catch her on foot. With her five-foot-five-inch small frame and long legs, Lacey was unmatched in speed; she was swift as a gazelle.

He heard the call over his new police scanner that a young college woman, who attended the same local university as Lacey, killed herself in her bathtub. It was the second suicide at the university within weeks, and Frank was convinced that his daughter was the cause. With Lacey's recent inheritance of speed and power along with the deaths that surrounded her, he knew he had to do whatever he needed to catch her and find a way to stop the horrible epidemic of death that began with him.

It was two o'clock in the morning on a chilly fall

Sunday in Michigan, the college parties were winding down and the downtown streets were near empty. Frank skidded around the corner of a barely lit street and saw no one. She was gone. He stopped the car and scoured every direction, then adjusted the black baseball cap that he religiously wore on his head. He rolled his window down to take a deep breath of the brisk air.

The sound of aluminum trashcans crashing to the ground in a nearby alley caught his attention. He raced to the alley to see Lacey bolt onto a road before he lost sight of her again.

The ground was wet from a recent downpour that left the moon's reflection in puddles covering the pavement. Lacey sprinted down another alley, splashing water over her already drenched body. Her breathing was heavy and her eyes were blood red and fierce. Strands of her dark stringy wet shoulder length hair plastered against her face.

Frank drove slowly down the narrow streets, peeking down alleys as he approached them. Finally, he saw a woman in a drunken stumble wearing a black thin raincoat over her black leggings and red flannel shirt. It was Lacey. She used the cement walls to keep her steady, and slowed her pace thinking she evaded her father until she saw the headlights from his car.

Lacey began in another sprint, not aware of the potholes that were camouflaged by the water. She stepped into one and tripped, causing her to fall to the ground, giving Frank time to screech upon her. He jumped out of his car and tackled her.

"Stop! Lacey! It's me, Dad!" he shouted with his raspy voice.

Lacey scuffled with the man, bellowing viciously as she threw him from her. She did not realize that he slipped his hand into the pocket of her coat, snatching a rag doll with orange yarn for hair and a sewn-on dress made of burlap. It was about five inches tall with no face and no details or definition to its hands and feet. He stood in exhaustion, ripped open the back of the doll held together with tacky adhesive and slid out a small wooden pen. Lacey abruptly stopped and gazed at the pen as if it controlled her. Then, in a rage, she lunged at him, pinning him against a brick wall. He was wide-eyed as she leaned in to his face.

"Lacey," he pleaded as the evil that radiated in her eyes sent chills through his bones.

She took hold of Frank's arm that held both the pen and the doll with a grip that was tight and painful. He could not keep grasp and dropped both into Lacey's hand.

"You can't stop this," she sneered with fury, pushing her stringy hair from her face and placing the pen back into the doll. "No one can."

"Lacey, listen to me. This is all my fault, you have to fight this, you still can."

She stepped away from him with a snarl.

"Don't do this!" he begged. "Don't let him win."

"It's done," she said. "This is what is meant for me and for him."

"This wasn't meant for you! I'm the poison in this world. What you're doing was meant for me!" he cried.

Lacey's pupils sparkled as crisp and clear as a diamond while the blood from her blown vessels continued to cover the whites of her eyes. With all her power, she whirled the flimsy doll into the air. Frank watched it fly over a chain link fence and into the back of an old pickup truck that was passing by. He stood in disbelief and despair as the truck faded from his view before he focused on his daughter who was in a daze. The sparkles disappeared from her pupils and her eyes became white.

"My journey is almost complete," Lacey said with rejoice, drawing a four-inch knife from her inside coat pocket.

"Please," Frank begged. "Don't do this."

At that moment, she thrust the knife into her abdomen. Frank ran to her, catching her before she landed on the ground. He caressed her lifeless face and began to sob.

"What have I done?"

CHAPTER TWO

Twelve-year-old Riley Rucker was always referred to as an explosion of energy by her friends and family. She started hip-hop dancing when she was five and spent all of her free time practicing her routines on the front lawn that spanned a half acre. She yanked her earbuds from her ears and proudly beamed when she saw her ten-year-old brother, Dylan, strolling to her.

"Our team is going to kill it next month. I can hardly wait to perform," Riley said with excitement. "Watch this!"

Riley's small frame and under average weight made it easy to jump and flip, but with her high energy, it was sometimes overpowering. She pushed her thick dark hair that fell to her shoulders, behind her ears and began her routine. She immediately twisted her foot in the wrong direction and landed on the ground.

"Is falling on your face part of the routine?" Dylan

asked with sarcasm.

Riley snarled at him and said, "I thought I had this part figured out, I can't let the team down, I gotta get it right."

"Can I watch?" Dylan asked.

"Only if you aren't going to joke and laugh."

"I won't."

Riley took a deep breath, crammed her earbuds in her pocket and dropped her phone on the grass. Hip-hop music played loudly as she danced to the beat, showing off the toned muscles in her legs.

"What do you think? I wish we had more than five minutes, we have a lot of tricks."

"It's good, I guess. What do I know?" Dylan replied.

Riley sighed and continued to dance while Dylan shook his head to the beat. Dylan glanced to the street to see a young boy on a bike with a basket of newspapers. As he reached their house, the boy hurled a newspaper at him, gliding past his arm.

"Hey, you little ass!" Riley yelled to the boy.

The boy gave a wink to Riley and sped into the street before noticing an old pickup truck coming upon him. The truck came to a screeching halt, missing the boy and throwing items from the truck to the side of the street. The boy continued to speed away on his bike while the driver, not realizing anything had fallen from the truck, began its journey again down the street.

Riley noticed the trash thrown from the truck and hurried into the street where a flimsy doll laid in the gutter. She lifted the doll in curiosity and examined it.

Dylan picked up the newspaper and approached Riley with a sour expression on his face. "What a creepy doll," he said.

Riley continued to examine the doll, brushing dirt from it.

"It's odd. Kinda cute."

"What's cute about it? Someone tried to make a doll and failed."

"I'm going to put it with my collection."

"Mom and Dad, especially Dad, aren't going to want it in your collection."

"Really Dylan? Dad barely notices anything we do," Riley said discouraged. "If he does have a problem with this doll that I plan on keeping, he'll have a fit for like ten minutes and then forget."

"I don't know about you, but that's what I like best about him. He's so into his job that if Mom's not home, we can do whatever we want," Dylan said with a chuckle.

"Have you ever noticed how our friend's dads act when they go to their games or even school performances?"

Dylan shrugged his shoulders and sat on the lawn.

"My friends get hugs from their dads, they get the whole 'you're great' or 'you're beautiful' and even 'I'm proud of you'. What have we ever gotten, if he even shows up? We get barely a high five but always get 'I gotta get back to the office' or whatever he has going on," Riley whined, sitting on the lawn beside him.

"It doesn't bother me. Not one bit," said Dylan. "Plus, he always makes up for it in gifts or cash, which I am totally cool with."

"Are you going to tell me that it never ever bothered you? Ever? If he were my real dad, it would bother me more," she said with sadness.

Dylan plucked at the grass. "He doesn't treat me any different. Get over it, if he stopped working to hang out with us more, we'd be broke," Dylan said, trying to cheer her up.

"It would be great if he put us before his work even a little. Seriously, I had to tell him a million times about the national competition and that we were counting on him to help with transportation. Every parent stepped up with all the other competitions but him."

Dylan chuckled, "Are you kidding? True, he forgot and now he can't be there, but he is renting this awesome bus to take everyone. It'll be fun."

"I'd rather have him there like the rest of the dads," said Riley in disappointment.

"Come on back inside," Dylan said, using Riley's shoulder as support to stand. He brushed grass from the back of his jeans. "Mom and Dad gave Ashley money to take us shopping after breakfast for new clothes."

As Dylan jogged back to the house, Riley noticed an older model black SUV parked a few yards down the street facing her. The windows were dark, even on the windshield and she could not see through the tint, but she dismissed it and went into the house with the doll.

Two men, both in their late thirties, dressed in jeans and black t-shirts, sat in the SUV watching Riley as she strolled to the back of the house and out of sight.

Stanley sat in the passenger seat. He was an unsavory man with a scraggly beard and a skinny frame, who obviously did not put hygiene as a lifestyle priority. He was high strung and anxiously pulled and twisted the hair on his chin with his fingers.

"Next time she comes out, let's do it," he quickly and impatiently said, vigorously rubbing his tattooed hands together.

Straight-faced Troy was behind the steering wheel acting calm and composed, holding a lit cigarette in his hand. He was clean-shaven and had short dark hair with hints of gray. He frequently scratched his lantern jaw with his thumb.

"Keep your cool, Stanley," he said. His voice was deep and he spoke slowly. "We need to wait for the old man and his wife to leave. That is, if you got your facts straight."

"I got 'em straight man. I know everything about this family. Rucker Architects, been around for fifteen years and since then, it has grown fast. Twenty-five offices in fifteen years, this guy must be loaded," Stanley stated. "Today, they will be leaving soon for a hob knob brunch. The kids will be home alone. Well almost."

"What else you got on him? Checking to see if you did your homework, we can't afford any surprises," said Troy, peering at the Rucker's yard.

"Married eleven years ago to Quinn. She's quite the plain Jane, but cute. Probably got married because he knocked her up with that boy, Dylan. Let's see, one stepchild, Riley. The kids are very active. Too hard to snatch either of them from one of their games or events, the mom is always hovering over them. Dad on the other hand shows up late, but he's mostly in his office that is as big as your apartment, until at least midnight. And what do I do? I wait and wait for him to get his ass out so that I can clean it," Stanley added as he got himself worked up. "I greet him as he's leaving and he'll grunt a 'hey' or 'how are ya', even though all he is probably thinking is 'what a low life'."

Troy laughed. "You are a low life which is why we are here. And you get an A on your homework. Very impressive, you didn't even need notes."

"Why not an A+?" Stanley asked in humor.

"Don't push it, I doubt you ever got an A in school, if

you even went."

"Been working for the bastard for six months. He doesn't even know I exist," said Stanley in a bitter tone. "He's such a pompous asshole that..."

"Everything will go as planned. I don't want us jumping the gun," Troy said, tossing his cigarette butt out the window. He leaned back in the seat and sighed.

"I'd give anything to have my own pad and this is going to make that happen. Don't get me wrong, your apartment is great Troy, and I owe you for taking me in like you did."

"Your luck is changing, starting with your old cell mate who was first, my cell mate. I owed him for having my back and to my surprise, he cashes in with a request to help you out. You're one lucky bastard."

Stanley continued to show his anxiousness. He glanced around the neighborhood examining the custom-built multi-million dollar homes, generously spaced apart from the other.

"Can you believe this house? It probably has at least ten bedrooms. What a life for a classic asshole."

Troy removed another cigarette from the pack that sat on the dashboard and lit it.

"Relax," Troy said, noticing Stanley's eagerness.

"I want what's coming to me. Roaming the halls and watching that man in his thousand dollar suits, while I clean up his and everybody else's shit from the toilets... that's all we exist for in his eyes," Stanley grunted. "And he sits on his throne nodding his head. I hate him."

"Can't hate who you don't know my friend. You hate your situation versus his. My job is as bad as yours is but you don't see me whining. At least not out loud."

"Whatever Troy. I'd rather break bricks and do hard

labor for a contractor than what I do. And don't you dare stand up for that guy. Don't!"

"I'm not. You're getting yourself all flustered for nothing. Chill out. It's time for Mr. Rucker to share the wealth. If you don't want it taken away, don't flaunt it. That's what I say."

Stanley gave a giddy grin. "I like that! This better go off as perfect as you say, 'cause I'm not leaving without getting paid and I ain't going back to jail."

"I get it! Enough already!" Troy shouted. "You've studied his every move for a long time. I know what I'm doing and I'm not going back either. This is gonna put us at the top my man."

Stanley snapped his fingers repeatedly with a grin.

"I'm going to take a vacation, like a forever vacation. And I'm gonna get my own car. A nice one like the rich people drive!" Stanley said in excitement.

"Gotta grab the goods first. Don't go spending what we don't have. How about we spend what we do have on some food. I'm hungry," said Troy, starting the engine. "I saw a burger place a few miles back. It won't take long," he said, making a U-turn and driving away.

CHAPTER THREE

Riley came into the spacious modern chefs' kitchen with the doll, where her rambunctious brother had started prepping to make pancakes. Riley laughed at his constant spilling of the batter from the bowl and stepped in to help him.

Ashley, the kid's cousin, watched the chaos. She was a skinny young woman in her early twenties and lived with the family to help around the house while she attended college. She gathered her shoulder length brunette hair into a ponytail, noticing the doll on the counter next to Riley. She appeared disgusted.

"Riley, where on earth did you get that? Find the trash, now," she ordered.

"I can't believe you brought it in," Dylan snickered, picking the doll up from the counter. "This is gross! Not even those stores that sell defective stuff would take this."

Dylan threw the doll on the floor and stomped on it while he laughed. Riley became angry and shoved him against the wall.

"I was just kidding!" Dylan yelled.

"Knock it off you guys!" Ashley ordered.

"It wasn't funny Dylan! Keep your smelly hands away from my things!"

Riley picked the doll up and calmed herself.

"She will go great with my collection. I have to keep her. Ashley, do you think she would survive the washing machine?"

"I think you need to throw it away, it is old and worn. If it fell out of a truck, then whoever had it last didn't want it. Plus, it would probably fall apart in the washing machine. Your mom and dad paid a lot of money for the cause of your doll collection, I don't think they..."

Gavin Rucker was average in appearance. He was a self-absorbed man in his late-forties who stood nearly six feet with a slender build. He strolled into the kitchen from an open hallway dressed in casual but tailored khakis and a polo shirt. An equally well-dressed woman, Quinn, followed behind him wearing a modest dress and low heels. She was a stay-at-home mom who carried a timid and submissive personality.

"Don't think they what?" questioned Gavin.

Gavin was a brilliant commercial architect, the deep wrinkles across his forehead and under his eyes showed evidence of the stress he carried with building his empire.

"Good morning everyone," Quinn greeted, adjusting her dress around her shapely hips.

"Riley's got a new, disgusting friend," said Dylan.

Gavin and Quinn glanced at Riley who was still holding the doll while Dylan giggled.

"Dylan, stop," she calmly said. "Riley, wha'cha got?"

Riley walked to her parents and raised the doll.

"She fell out of a truck," Riley innocently replied.

"It was Mr. Ballard's truck," Dylan added. "He was probably coming from the house on the end picking up junk."

"It's bad enough that he drives that piece of shit up and down our streets, now he's losing it off the back?"

Riley became bitter. "He was trying to avoid the paper boy who ran in front of him. And what would you do with your junk if you didn't have someone as nice as Mr. Ballard to come and pick it up? Who cares what he drives?"

"Wow. I didn't know we resort to dumpster diving," said Gavin.

"Not everything has to be brand new with a ridiculous price. I'm keeping this doll."

"You have plenty of dolls sitting in a very expensive display case, I hope you're not going to add that thing to your collection," said Gavin. He looked at Quinn. "What's wrong with this kid?"

"I collect all kinds of dolls! What's wrong with that?" Riley shouted.

"Riley, keep the doll," Quinn said in the same calm manner, gathering her long hair and wrapping it in a bun. "It's no big deal Gavin."

"It's a big deal if someone sees it," said Gavin, insulted.

"Good grief," Riley said under her breath.

"Yeah, I heard that Riley and my thoughts exactly," said Gavin, mocking her. "Good grief."

"Gavin. Really?" Quinn leaned to Riley's ear and whispered, "Put it in your room, he'll forget that you even have it."

Quinn winked at Riley, she winked back before walking out of the kitchen.

"Quinn. Really?" he mocked again with displeasure.

Quinn continued in her relaxed demeanor, "Let it go."

"You spoil her, you spoil both of them," said Gavin, rudely. "You know what? Forget it. We have to get going."

"Romantic brunch for you two?" Ashley playfully asked.

"We are going to meet one of Gavin's potential clients out at the golf course," said Quinn, trying to hide that she was unhappy.

Ashley's grin faded. "I'll grab the kids something at the mall for lunch."

"Ashley, you are such a lifesaver," Quinn sincerely said. "How long before school starts?"

"No, you and Gavin are the lifesavers. If my wonderful uncle hadn't opened your home to me, I would have never been able to afford to go to school out here. Out of state tuition is insane. And school doesn't start for another week. I'm so glad we start later than the other schools."

"Make it worth your while Ashley, don't screw up," Gavin grumbled. "Not everyone gets a chance like you have, and on that note, we gotta go."

"Can I stay home? I want to keep practicing?" Riley begged.

"And can I go over to Aaron's?" Dylan asked with excitement.

Ashley chuckled. "What? Neither of you want to go shopping with your favorite aunt for new clothes? Who are you two?"

"Riley, you can stay, don't leave the yard. And as for

you young man," Quinn said, gently placing her hands on the boy's round face. "No, you can't go over to Aaron's. You're still grounded for lighting off those illegal fireworks. You're stuck with Ashley today."

She skimmed her hand over the top of Dylan's oily head, and then wiped her hand on a towel. "You need to wash that dirty hair."

"Let's go Quinn, I don't want to be late," Gavin barked.

Quinn rolled her eyes to Ashley who chuckled.

"Ready," she replied, forcing a smile and following Gavin out the door to their black Mercedes that sat in the driveway.

They hopped in and drove around the horseshoe curve and out onto the road. The SUV was still gone.

Quinn was already dreading the half hour drive to the golf course to meet with Gavin's potential clients. Gavin was hungry to raise the bar of his own success and nothing else seemed to matter. Every drive alone with him was more painful than the last, and over the years, the more success he gained, the more unbearable he became. His overinflated ego had completely taken over. Nothing was ever positive with him and he vocalized his frustrations to her on every drive. She ignored his flaws, until recently when she started to feel that she and the kids were nothing but a burden.

After losing her first husband and Riley's biological father to cancer, she never imagined ever falling in love again, especially with someone like Gavin. She met him at a silent auction where she was working as an assistant event planner. It was love at first sight for him and he was patient for Quinn to spark the same feelings. She evaded him for weeks while he showered her office with roses, chocolates and greeting cards, often sending toys to Riley. Quinn finally let her guard down and while skeptical, she had fallen in love with him.

Riley was too young to remember her father, but Quinn displayed a photo of him in her bedroom and talked often to her about who he was. Once married to Gavin, he insisted she quit her job, and because her need to please was stronger than her need for independence, she left her job.

As the years passed, instead of her excitement to accompany Gavin wherever he went, she counted the minutes and the miles to when she could escape the misery of being locked in a car with him. She never gave her opinion to her husband mainly because it was never the same as his, and his demeaning words trained her to keep silent.

The highlight of any business lunch or dinner was that Quinn could indulge in fine food and barely listen to the conversations of sales strategies and whatever revenue goals they had. It was beyond boring, and with every meeting, she found herself counting whatever was on her plate. This time it was the chopped tomatoes in her marinara sauce over her frittata. She ate as slow as she could, trying to calculate the end of the meeting with the end of her meal.

Riley's home was the envy of her friends, especially her bedroom that was the hot spot for sleepovers. She didn't live near her school or her friends, but none seemed to mind the fifteen-mile drive to visit her. The Rucker house was nestled in a rural neighborhood where several expensive colonial homes sat.

She wasn't excessive with tidiness, but she did like order to her room, especially her collection of dolls that sat in a tall custom-made wooden case that stood over half the height of her twelve-foot ceilings.

Her dolls, from all over the world, were carefully stacked on glass shelves and in perfect rows. She started collecting dolls at five years old when she went to Tokyo with her family. Her mother bought her a porcelain doll that mesmerized her, and ever since, the features and the details in the design of the dolls would captivate her. She didn't travel to other countries often, but when she did, she always found a doll that would allow her imagination to roam and take her through many adventures.

Riley never played with her collection. They went straight from its packaging to her case where she spent hours staring and studying each one. Gavin traveled occasionally and wherever he went, he would bring her a doll. Gavin's generosity to her with new dolls was one of the few connections that she had with him.

She laid on her bed cleaning the doll that she had found with a cloth. She grinned while watching the stains disappear as she rubbed the front of it. She jumped from her bed and strolled down the stairs with the doll under her arm and into the kitchen. Ashley and Dylan were getting ready to leave.

"Are you sure you don't wanna go? It'll be fun, new clothes," Ashley asked, trying to entice her.

"Pick something for me. I have to keep practicing until I get the whole routine right," Riley said, holding up the doll. "All cleaned up."

"I still think it's ugly," uttered Dylan.

"Let's go Dylan, we have a lot of stops," said Ashley as she opened the kitchen door that led to the garage.

"Remember Riley, you are not to leave the yard. There's deli meat in the fridge for a sandwich if you get hungry."

Moments after Ashley and Dylan left, not seeing that the SUV was parked once again on the street, Riley trotted out of the house with the doll in her hand. When she reached the front lawn, she sat it down and began her dance routine.

Troy and Stanley's faces brightened when they saw Riley appear. Troy was smug. He threw his partially smoked cigarette out of the window and shoved the SUV in gear.

"All good things," Troy said with determination. "We are lucky only the boy left."

"Yes! Let's do this!" Stanley said in excitement as he practically inhaled fries.

The SUV slowly rolled into the Rucker's driveway through the opened gate. Riley turned off her music from her phone that was snug in her dance pants and picked up her doll. Troy exited the driver side of the vehicle with a map under his arm, his demeanor was unsuspecting. He adjusted his jeans for a better fit over his beer gut while Riley stood on the opposite side of the SUV peering over the hood at him. She peeked in the passenger side and saw the silhouette of Stanley.

"Hi," he cheerfully greeted. "Is Peter home?"

"I'm sorry, you have the wrong house. No Peter here."

Troy scratched his face, and then said, "Is this 45287 West Oakleigh Place?"

"No this is Drive. Oakleigh Place is on the other side of the main road."

Troy walked around to the passenger side and stood in front of her. He showed her the map.

"Any chance you can point us?"

"Sure, but your phone probably gives better directions."

"We're a bit old school, probably just old compared to you. Those phones are over our heads," Troy chuckled.

Riley laughed as she stood beside Troy. "Let me see your map."

As she examined the map, Troy carefully pulled a syringe from his back pocket and quickly injected it into Riley's neck, giving her no time to react or realize what had happened. She immediately passed out, dropping the doll at her feet.

Troy quickly but gently slid her into the back seat of the SUV. He picked the doll up from the ground, threw it on her and slammed the door shut. He trotted back to the driver side, glancing in all directions before hopping in and driving away.

It was late afternoon, Gavin and Quinn walked into the house from the garage door that led to the kitchen. Ashley and Dylan walked in with their hands full with shopping bags.

"Hello!" Dylan cheerfully greeted, showing off the shopping bags. "I think I wore Ashley completely out. I'm glad I went. I got a bunch of new t-shirts for school. I gotta show Riley what we picked out for her."

"After the issue with that doll she found, I figured Dylan could pick a few extra things for her. As a truce, though they probably both already forgot about it," said Ashley.

"I hope she didn't put that disgusting doll in her

display case. Dylan, check to see that she threw it out," he called to him as he whisked past with the shopping bags.

"How was brunch?" Ashley asked. "After we hit every shop in the mall, Dylan and I tried out this new restaurant outside the mall. You'll have to try it."

"Sure. And the brunch was... long. But I think Gavin landed a new client. I'm so proud of him."

"Thank you, thank you," Gavin proudly replied, giving Quinn a kiss on her cheek. "Next time, try to at least act like you are interested. A few words from my biggest fan would have been nice."

He kissed her again, not seeing her roll her eyes. "Ashley, thanks for taking at least one of your cousins shopping. I'll be in my den."

Gavin walked past Dylan who was hurrying back to the kitchen.

"She's not up there," Dylan said, catching Gavin's attention.

Gavin became annoyed. "She was not to leave the yard," he said.

"Hm, did Riley say if she was going anywhere before you left?" Quinn asked.

"I told her to stay in the yard if she was going outside," Ashley added.

"Well, she's not up there," said Dylan.

Quinn pulled her cell phone from her purse and called Riley's phone that went directly to voice mail.

"That's odd, she's not answering. She would never let her battery die, let alone turn it off."

"Ashley, Dylan, you two go check around the neighborhood. Quinn, try calling some of her friends," Gavin calmly directed.

CHAPTER FOUR

Riley was regaining consciousness. She was disoriented. When she opened her eyes, everything was a blur. She slowly lifted her pounding head, noticing that her vision was clearing and she was able to see that she was in an old run-down cabin with layers of cobwebs hanging from every corner. The sofa she laid on in a fetal position was old and smelled of must. Other than the disgusting furniture where she laid, there were two old rusted lawn chairs in the middle of the room with a wooden television tray between them. A small kitchenette housed a toaster oven, an old cast iron skillet and a few utensils that sat on the dust covered counter. Several empty fast food bags and wrappers were scattered about the floor.

Riley was too frightened to move from the couch, even though no one was there. She frowned and rubbed her face, noticing the doll beside her.

"How did I get here? Where am I?" she softly cried.

She could hear the murmur of male voices outside. It was Troy and Stanley who leaned against the SUV parked to the side of the cabin that was mostly hidden by brush and weeds. Troy lit a cigarette and inhaled deeply with each puff.

"Make sure you put that thing out," Stanley ordered. "Last thing we need is a fire blowing our plans."

"Don't worry about my ashes. I have it covered," Troy responded, annoyed that Stanley dared to tell him what to do. "You need to worry about keeping that kid in order until this is done."

"And I got that covered," said Stanley. "Are you taking that slut of a girlfriend away with you after this is all over?"

"Call her what you want, you couldn't even pay a street walker to be with you. No fun exploring Mexico alone."

"I'll find me a real beauty when I cross the border. No fun dragging baggage."

They both chuckled.

"She's gotta be coming to by now. We better check on her," Stanley added.

The front door to the cabin swung open and the men walked in. The creaking of the wood floor along with the hoof sounds from their boots made Riley more frightened. Both stood in front of the terrified girl who fiercely clung to the doll. Stanley grinned at her with dollar signs practically beaming from his eyes.

"Wh... why did you bring me here?" Riley whimpered.

"Don't you worry your pretty little head about that," said Troy as he slowly paced around the small room. "As long as your daddy does what we tell him, you'll be home before you know it."

"I... I want to go home now," Riley demanded, holding back tears.

Troy glanced at Stanley and then back to the petrified child. "Let me see what I can do about that. I'm going to take a drive into town and pick up a few things, maybe even get you something to eat," he said. "While I'm out and have reception, I'll be making a call, and the outcome of that will determine when you get to go home."

"If you get to go home," Stanley added in a pompous manner.

"I have to go to the bathroom," said Riley, still holding tightly to the doll.

"Go take her and don't move one step from the door while she is in there. I'll be back in a couple hours," he said to Stanley.

Stanley reached down and firmly grasped Riley by her arm, pulling her up. She continued to hold the doll as he practically dragged her to the bathroom. He pushed her in and slammed the door.

"Don't take all day."

Riley caught herself against the wall, dropping the doll to her feet. As she reached down to pick it up, she saw an opening in the doll's fabric, barely noticeable and fastened with tacky adhesive. She opened it and saw a small pen tucked inside. It was a thick dull wooden pen, about two inches long, with several nicks all around. She yanked the pen from the fabric, studying every part of it. She then sat the doll on the dirty basin of the sink and placed the tip of the pen on it. She began scribbling the dark and thick ink over the arm of the doll when she was startled by loud banging on the door by Stanley.

"Hurry up!"

As Riley lifted the pen from the doll, the ink began to leak from a pin-sized hole down to her skin, between her first finger and thumb, leaving four tattooed lines, one longer than the rest. As if she was jolted, Riley gasped. Her eyes bulged, immediately blowing her blood vessels. Her hazel pupils shined a shimmer of light that quickly disappeared along with the blood in her eyes. She had a devious manner about her as she quietly and carefully examined the marks on her hand. She sniffed a few times noticing an enhanced sense of smell before glancing around the room and at the rusted sink and toilet. She stared at herself in the partially broken mirror and deeply inhaled and exhaled.

Without using the toilet, she put the pen in the pocket of her pants and tucked the doll under her arm. She swung the door open and gave a piercing glare that made Stanley uneasy. The intimidation and terror that she originally felt was gone. He reached for her arm and she quickly snatched away, storming back to the couch.

It had been two hours since Riley's disappearance. Quinn called every parent of Riley's friends with no luck. No one had seen her. Quinn was sitting on the couch frazzled and rocking uncontrollably when Ashley and Dylan walked in the door.

"I'm scared, she's nowhere," said Ashley in to tears. "We can't find her, we drove everywhere."

"We have to call the police," Quinn ordered to Gavin who had already made his way to the house phone that sat on the kitchen island.

As he reached for the phone, it rang, showing Riley's number on the screen.

"It's Riley!" he announced to everyone before going back to the call. "Riley what the hell, you had us worried sick, where are..."

"Whoa whoa daddy," Troy calmly said.

He was parked in a small shopping center standing outside his vehicle, casually leaning against the door. He flicked a cigarette butt from his hand to the ground.

"Who is this and why do you have my daughter's phone? Where is she?" Gavin bellowed.

"She's real cute, Riley that is. She's as cute as that adorable boy, Dylan. Mama Quinn makes adorable babies. You have the perfect wealthy family. And Ashley, she's a bit plain, but with a bit of imagination, she could be a real hottie."

"How much?" Gavin asked, trying to stay calm. "I'll give you what you want and you will return her unharmed, end of story. Now, how much?"

Quinn reacted to Gavin's words and quickly stood behind him trying to listen in on the call. "Someone has Riley?"

Gavin lifted his hand, waving for her to be silent.

"Are you still there? Hello. I want to talk to her," Gavin ordered, crimping his thin lips.

"No cops or you will be talking to her from her grave."

"What do you want?" Gavin yelled, clinching his teeth.

Quinn, in panic, said to Ashley, "Take Dylan upstairs."

"Mom," Dylan said. "What's going on?"

"Go! Now! Please!" Quinn yelled, causing both Ashley and Dylan to scurry away. "Gavin, talk to me! What's happened?"

With the receiver still at Gavin's ear, he waved her silent again.

"The clock's ticking and ticking away your little girl's life. I want two million big ones. Two million dollars, in cash. My gosh!" he yelled in joy. "I don't even know how many briefcases that is!" He laughed and continued, "Of course you'll say you don't have that kind of money on you and the banks are closed. Here is what I am going to do to keep you in line. I'll keep your little prize, unharmed, until tomorrow. On Monday, at noon, I want my money. Not Tuesday or the day after but Monday, tomorrow."

Gavin was frozen for a moment and unable to speak a word. He covered the mouth of the phone.

"He wants two million dollars by noon tomorrow and says he's not going to let her go until he gets the money."

"What?" Quinn said in shock. "No! You gotta get her back now!"

Gavin spoke helplessly into the phone again, "I'll get the money... Tonight. I want her back tonight."

Troy lit another cigarette, taking his time to speak again into the phone. He blew out a puff of smoke and said, "That's what I like to hear! Now that you've played your hand, let's get this over with. Since you seem to be able to exceed my expectations, I'm going to let you pick the time while I pick the location."

"Midnight, now tell me where," Gavin quickly answered, feeling a lump in his throat. He rubbed his hand over his thin hair and receding hairline.

"Woodman Highway, take the last exit and go all the way down to where it ends. It's always deserted, except for at midnight that is. Once I have the cash, I will tell you where to pick up your kid."

"No, you bring her with you or no deal."

"How about I kill her now," Troy quickly blurted.

There was silence on both ends as Gavin contemplated his next move.

Troy spoke slowly, emphasizing every word. "Bring the cash and you will get her back," he said, before abruptly ending the call.

Gavin spent a moment staring at the clock on the wall. His heart was racing and he could feel every beat pounding through his ears.

"We need to call the police, Gavin," demanded Quinn in a panic. She interlocked her fingers, squeezing them together as tight as she could.

"No. We can't risk Riley's life and the last thing I want is the publicity."

Quinn became hysterical. "I don't care about publicity! You can't drive out there alone!"

"They will kill her Quinn! We can't call the police! I have to do this!"

"What if they don't give her back? We won't win! I know it!"

"Let me think! Let me think for a minute. I said I will get her back," he said, putting both hands on her shoulders to comfort her. "I promise."

###

Troy drove back to the cabin and walked inside where Stanley stood, perplexed in front of Riley who was sitting like a statue. Her face was blank and they could hear her quick and heavy breaths.

"What's wrong with her?" Troy asked.

"Don't know," said Stanley. "Maybe it's some rich person meditation ritual that keeps them from flipping out. Who knows?"

"As long as she stays quiet."

"Should we tie her up?" Stanley asked.

"Nah, she's not moving. She's like a mannequin," said Troy with a chuckle.

"You made the call, what's next?" Stanley asked, still watching the girl whose eyes were staring through the walls. He scratched his head. "She's weird."

Stanley moved one of the lawn chairs closer to Riley and sat.

"Sounds like we are about to become rich boys at midnight."

Stanley chuckled. "You're kidding. He actually has two million dollars on him?"

"He does and that's what I call really wanting to get this kid back. We will be out of here sooner than we planned."

"I'm getting that Porsche!" Stanley exclaimed.

A jolt went through Riley's body like electricity that drew her from her trance. Her head began to twitch as her eyes rolled back into her head. She tightly squeezed her eyes, trying to withstand the feeling as she dropped down on the couch and curled in the fetal position with the doll in her arms.

Stanley stood and approached Troy who was standing near the front door.

"What the hell is going on with this girl? She's spazzing out, I mean literally and she's freaking me out. You know we can't send her back home. She's seen our faces. She'll rat us out and you know it," Stanley whispered.

"I'm not ready to kill anyone. She's not going to say a word, especially if we emphasize that we can snatch her or her brother any time we wanted if she were to tell. As soon as we get the money, we let her go."

"I don't know, it's risky."

"Trust me, people like this aren't going to say a word."

Stanley sighed and walked away from him.

"What are you going to do? What are you thinking?" Quinn asked Gavin in tears.

Gavin picked up his cell phone and made a call.

"Jack, I need you to pull two million for me... just do it. Yes, two million, marked... Three hours? ... Okay. Meet me at the office, I need your help," he said before ending the call and embracing Quinn. "You've got to keep it together. I'm going to get her back. Stay here, don't tell Dylan or Ashley anything else and don't call the police."

Quinn shook her head. She rubbed her trembling hands together as she watched her husband hurry down the hall to his den where he stepped in to compose himself and collect his thoughts. Shortly after, Gavin found himself racing down the freeway, and with very little traffic and excessive speed, his normal two-hour commute ended at ninety minutes. He briskly walked through the corridor of his firm and to his lavish office where he met Jack, a white older thick built man wearing loose jeans, a blue dress shirt and black sneakers.

"Did you get it?" Gavin asked out of breath.

"Over there boss. All marked as you requested," Jack answered, pointing to two black duffel bags. "What's going on? Obviously someone has something on you. Problem with one of the executives competing on this bid? I know it's a big one. I can make it go away, just like before. Who do we need to deliver it to?"

"Some bastard took Riley and is demanding two million dollars."

"Let me and my men take care of this," Jack confidently and sternly said.

"I contracted you to keep an eye on my powerful competition and handle my discreet financial matters. This is certainly out of your job description, at least with me."

"But you know I'm capable and this does fall under 'financial' matters."

"No, I can't risk it and you are to tell no one, understand? This bid means everything. I won't have anything, and I mean anything clouding it."

Gavin grabbed one of the bags and headed to the door. "Get the other one and follow me."

Jack snatched the bag from the floor and hustled out the door with Gavin to his car. They threw the bags in the trunk.

"Gavin, are you sure about this? This asshole sounds like an amateur. I can handle this. At least let me go with you."

"I'm sure. Listen, I know I sound insensitive. I'm not pitting my kid against my company, I swear that's not what I'm doing, but this could have a negative impact on my firm."

He spent a moment, glaring at the bags sitting in his trunk.

"How did I not see this coming? My family means everything to me. If I go to the police, it could cost Riley her life. I should have spent more time keeping my family safe. This is all my fault."

"I get it Gavin. You're going to get through this and

get her back, and then we make some changes that will protect your family going forward."

"You told me something like this could happen and I ignored you," said Gavin, slamming the trunk shut. "Do what you have to in order to keep my family safe. Keep this quiet. I'm making the drop at midnight and I need to get going. It'll take me another hour and a half, maybe longer to get there. And I am going to take you up on your offer. Once I have her home, I'll give you the go for you to find my money and to take care of this bastard."

Gavin hurried into his car and sped away. His anxiety increased with every red light that caught him and was relieved to have finally gotten on the near empty freeway. He took the exit as instructed and drove on a curvy two-lane road for a few more miles until he reached the dead end. He stopped the car, popped the trunk and stepped out into the night and to the back of the car that was illuminated by the bright moon. He was nervous and scared as he thought about every way this could go wrong. He saw headlights from a vehicle parked in the dirt about fifty yards away. The headlights flashed on and then off. Gavin took the bags from the trunk and dropped them to the ground.

Troy sat comfortably in his SUV with a lit cigarette dangling from his lips. He peered through the windshield watching as Gavin sat the bags on the ground. Gavin glanced to the SUV one last time before climbing back into his car. After another minute, he drove away, praying he had done the right thing and he soon would see Riley again.

Troy snagged the cigarette from his mouth and held it between his fingers as he began his slow drive to the bags.

"Hello pay day," he said with satisfaction.

CHAPTER FIVE

Troy was amazed at how smooth his plan was going. He had two million dollars sitting beside him and was back at the cabin. He stepped out of the SUV carrying the bags and opened the door to the cabin. A lone, bare light bulb hung from the ceiling brightly lighting up the room. Stanley stood in front of Riley watching her as she trembled. She balled her fists and began to moan.

"Let's pack it up. Pay day has arrived," Troy said in excitement before noticing the girl. "What's going on? Now what's wrong with her?"

"She's been like this since you left. I think she's sick man."

"Get her up. We'll let her go along the freeway. In a couple days we pick up our new ID's and passports then get the hell out of dodge," said Troy, unconcerned with what was happening to the girl.

He whisked through the room gathering things and

throwing one of the bags across the floor to Stanley. "That one is yours."

Stanley stopped it with his foot and quickly opened it. "Sweet! Hello Porsche!"

Troy grinned. "Let's take the kid and..."

Troy was interrupted by Riley abruptly sitting up and convulsing, following with a screech.

"You can't stop it! You can't stop him!" she cried before gasping then falling limp onto the couch.

"What the...?" Stanley said, cautiously approaching the girl, examining her with his eyes. "I don't think she is breathing."

Troy walked to Riley and raised her wrist. He checked for a pulse before dropping her arm.

"Damn it," he said. "Pick her up and let's get out of here. It'll be never to forever before anyone finds her out here," Troy said with no emotion. "This ain't our problem."

"And what are we supposed to do with her now? We can't get caught with a dead kid."

Troy shrugged his shoulders. "There's a shovel out back. Bury her out past the property line. There's a bunch of junk that's been there forever, and don't forget that damn doll. We'll lay low at the apartment. One last rent payment for us. "

Stanley lifted the girl with the doll. "You get the shovel," he said, struggling to carry Riley out of the back door. "You know, this is for the best. She probably would have ratted us out."

"Whatever man," Troy said, walking to the back door and opening it.

###

The sun was rising. It had been hours since Gavin dropped off the ransom money, yet still no Riley. Ashley and Dylan were weary, and neither could sleep. They sat outside on the porch until it became morning. Quinn was on the verge of madness. She anxiously paced the floor from the kitchen, past the curved staircase, through the foyer to the front door and back. She had enough, the thought of what could be happening to Riley was tearing at her gut. She dashed to the kitchen table and reached for the telephone. Gavin firmly set his hand over hers.

"We've been waiting all night! I'm not going to stand here and do nothing! They still have her! This wasn't the deal!" she cried as the front door burst open.

Ashley and Dylan walked in with Riley who was covered in dirt. She was quiet, emotionless and no longer carrying the doll.

"Mom!" Dylan yelled.

Quinn ran to Riley and wrapped her arms around her small frame, her eyes flooded with tears. Gavin peeked outside the door and saw nothing.

"Thank God you're here!" Quinn cried in joy before noticing Riley's strange demeanor.

Gavin hurried to Riley and hugged her. She promptly pushed him away.

"I'm okay Mom," Riley said softly as Quinn guided her to the sofa.

"Did you see how she got home?" he asked Dylan and Ashley.

"We saw her walking from the cul-de-sac," answered Dylan.

"Did you see a car?"

"No. Nothing," said Ashley.

"You two go upstairs," Quinn said. "We need to talk to Riley."

Riley sat between her parents on the sofa.

"Riley, what happened? Are you hurt?" Gavin asked.

Riley was callous to her dad. "No, they didn't hurt me," she said. "I'm dirty, I want to get cleaned up."

"How did you get the dirt all over you?" Quinn asked in a concerned tone. "Tell us what happened."

"I don't remember everything. I was outside practicing my routine. A guy came into the driveway and asked for directions with a map. The next thing I knew I was in this disgusting shack laying on a couch that smelled like animals peed all over it."

"Did you see who did this? How did you get home?" Gavin anxiously asked. "Any idea of where he was holding you?"

Quinn noticed the marks on Riley's right hand. She reached to her causing Riley to pull away and tuck her hands under her legs.

"What's on your hand? How did you get those marks?" Quinn asked, not giving her time to answer Gavin's questions. "Where did the dirt come from?"

Quinn began brushing it from her clothes and onto the floor while Riley remained silent.

"Maybe we should talk about this after I've gotten her cleaned up. Gavin, would you ask Ashley if she would fix a bowl of soup for her?"

"I'm not hungry," Riley quickly replied.

"Did they feed you?" Quinn asked.

"No," Riley said, becoming annoyed. "I'm not hungry."

"If you don't want it, you can eat it when you feel up to it," Gavin suggested.

Riley nodded. Gavin walked away to find Ashley while Quinn escorted Riley up the stairs, caressing her back as they walked. Riley did not utter a word the entire time Quinn was with her. She drew her bath and waited on Riley's bed until she was finished bathing and dressed. Riley slowly and quietly came out of the bathroom and climbed into her bed.

"Riley, Honey, I can stay with you if you would like."

"I want to sleep," she said, laying on her side with her back to Quinn.

"We will talk when you wake."

Quinn sat beside Riley for a moment, watching and rubbing her shoulder, noticing her erratic breathing. She leaned in and kissed her on her cheek and after another moment of watching her, she walked out, closing the door behind. She went back downstairs and joined Gavin on the sofa in the family room.

"Did she say anything?" Gavin asked.

"No. She wanted to go to sleep. I can't believe this is happening. What if he comes back and tries to do this again?"

"We have her back and he has his money. But I promise you, he won't get away with this. I'm taking care of it."

"I'm worried. She came in very calm, I mean eerie calm. She wasn't hysterical, no tears. Gavin, she wasn't upset at all."

Gavin chimed in, "I think she's in shock, wouldn't you be?"

"I guess but, it's strange," she claimed. "And how are you planning on taking care of this?"

"As soon as one dollar of that money is spent, Jack will know. Also, a couple of his men will be outside the house at all times," he said, standing. "Until this blows over, it's what we are going to do. I have work to finish," he said in a dismissive manner, walking away.

Gavin entered his den and sat at his desk. He picked up the telephone and dialed a number.

"Jack, this is Gavin. I know it's early. Riley's home... yes, she is fine. I don't have much to give you, I think it was an SUV, dark, probably black. It was too far for me to get any more than that... There could be more than one, I couldn't see... I want my money back and I don't care what you do to the bastard that orchestrated this, as long as he never does it again. Once we can talk to Riley more, I may have additional information, but do whatever you can, now."

Gavin disconnected the call, stood and walked out of his office to gather his family. Dylan and Ashley sat together on the couch while Gavin stood in front of them with Quinn who was grim.

"We know that somebody took Riley," said Dylan. "It's not like the walls are made of cement. Why aren't the police here?"

"We... We th..." Quinn tried to say.

Gavin approached Dylan and knelt. "We think it's best that we keep this quiet. Which means you two cannot talk about this to any of your friends."

Dylan gave a sad nod.

"I don't want you to worry. I have this handled," he said, checking his watch. "I have to go to a meeting at one of my sites, but I will be back as soon as I can."

Ashley was worried and curious about how Riley was feeling. She walked into her bedroom where Riley sat at the foot of her bed staring into space.

"Riley," Ashley said, creeping to her. "I wanted to see

how you were doing."

Riley said nothing. She closed her eyes as her body began to quiver, startling Ashley.

"Riley!" she yelled, placing her hands on her shoulders and shaking her. "What's the matter with you?"

She glanced at Riley's hand and noticed the tattooed bars. "What's this?" she asked, trying to examine it.

Riley snatched her hand away, then held her head as if she were hurting.

"I'm going to get your mom."

"No!" Riley shouted and then gasped.

Ashley ran to the door, then stopped.

"Os... Ost..." Riley sputtered. "Ostar, I'm almost ready."

"What?" Ashley questioned, daring to take a few steps towards her.

Riley keeled over in excruciating pain. "Ostar," she softly whimpered.

"Ostar? Who the heck is that? Is that who kidnapped you? Ostar who?"

"Ashley, go! Please! Leave!"

Ashley ran out of the room and down the stairs to Quinn who was sitting quietly at the kitchen table rubbing her forehead. She was torn as to what to do to the point that it paralyzed her.

"Quinn!" Ashley yelled.

Quinn snapped out of her bleakness. "What's wrong? Is it Riley?"

"Yes, come quick, something is wrong with her."

Quinn quickly followed Ashley up the stairs and into Riley's bedroom where she laid on her stomach facing the foot of her bed laughing as she watched a funny movie on her television. Ashley was confused.

"I swear, she was totally freaking out..."

Quinn sat on the edge of the bed.

"Riley, how are you feeling?" Quinn asked in a soothing tone.

Ashley was baffled.

"Freaking out? What are you talking about?" Riley laughed.

"Who is Ostar?" Ashley asked Riley then said to Quinn, "She said the name Ostar and that she was almost ready. Ready for what Riley?"

Riley shrugged her shoulders.

"We need to talk about what happened to you. Was the man who took you named Ostar?" Quinn asked, still calm.

Riley innocently looked at her mother, ignoring her question.

Quinn sighed. "I'm going to call the school and I'll talk to your dance coach. I'm going to keep you home for a few days."

"I don't need to go to school. They can't teach me anything I don't already know."

Ashley chuckled. "I doubt that Riley. What about the competition?"

"Who cares, they are all stupid."

Quinn arched her eyebrows. "You don't mean that. I have a great idea, you should give a couple of your friends a call. Might make you feel better."

Riley turned the television off, hopped from her bed and immediately became upset. "Damn it!"

"Riley!" scolded Quinn.

"Those bastards! They have my phone!" she yelled, filled with anger.

"Riley! Stop! Sit down!"

Riley calmed herself and sat next to her mother.

"They? How many were there?"

"Two," Riley quickly said.

"Did you see their faces? Would you recognize them if you saw them again?"

"I hate them," she said with a bitter tone. "What is going to be done to them?"

Ashley and Quinn were both hesitant to speak.

"Nothing? Gavin doesn't want to do anything?"

Quinn felt ashamed.

"Then why do I have to talk about it?"

Quinn placed both hands on Riley's shoulders. "Riley, this is hard to explain. Your dad loves you, he loves all of us, we need to trust him to handle this."

Riley rolled her eyes then gently pushed her mom's hands away from her and smiled. "I need a new phone. Will you get me a new one?"

Quinn, in concern, wrapped her arms around Riley. "Yes, of course, I'll order it today."

"Thank you. I think I want to take a shower. I still feel gross."

Ashley and Quinn watched in confusion as Riley stood, took clothes from her dresser and walked into her bathroom, closing the door behind her.

"Something is wrong with her."

"I know. I am going to get her to a doctor. It's hard getting an emergency appointment when you can't say it's an emergency," said Quinn with uncertainty. "But this has got to be extremely hard for her and it will take some time for her to be back to herself."

They could hear Riley humming on the other side of the door.

"Who is Ostar? She said it so weird," Ashley questioned. "It was like she was possessed."

"Are you sure of what you saw and that she said

Ostar? We are all functioning on fumes, I think it was
your imagination."

"It wasn't my imagination Quinn. She curled over like
she was in a lot of pain and then said that name. By the
time I got you, she was a totally different person," Ashley
claimed. "Did you notice that she called Gavin by his
name? And what's up with those stains on her hand?"

"Yes, I did notice and I don't know what to think
about the marks. I don't know what to think about any of
this."

"Do you think we should call the police? I know he's
my uncle but he's not always right. You know that."

"He's handling it, he said he is. We have to trust him."

Quinn stood, sighed and took Ashley's arm. "Come
on, let's leave her alone. Don't worry," she said, guiding
her out and gently closing Riley's door. "You need rest
Ashley."

Inside the bathroom, Riley stood in front of the
mirror staring at herself. When she heard the bedroom
door close, she came out and walked into her closet. She
found the dance pants she wore when she was kidnapped
in her laundry basket and reached into the pocket, pulling
out the pen that was inside the doll. She carefully studied
it as she walked to her desk.

Riley sat and began drawing on a piece of paper, not
noticing that the ink from the pen had run down to the
same spot on her hand as the last time. As soon as it
touched her skin, the stain became darker. She felt the
wind being knocked from her and she gasped for air,
falling to the floor. She laid on her back for a moment
before that same bright sparkle flashed in her pupils and
the whites of her eyes filled with blood. It disappeared as
she formed an eerie grin. She picked herself up from the

floor and went back to her desk.

CHAPTER SIX

Later that morning, Quinn sat on a bar stool at the kitchen island in deep thought, bothered by her own lack of action. She was never one to take the initiative to do anything that she felt was right, and now she struggled more than ever. She was too afraid and insecure to rely or trust her own judgment.

She sipped from her coffee cup watching Ashley, who had her back to her, washing the dishes. Gavin strolled in from his early meeting in a good mood, acting as if nothing happened.

"Where are the kids?" he asked.

Quinn remained preoccupied in thought and didn't initially hear her cheerful husband come in.

Ashley noticed Quinn, then spoke, "Dylan wanted to go to school to be with his friends. Riley's in her room."

"I'll have a couple men from my security keep an eye

on Dylan. They will also be discreet when they are outside the house."

"For how long?" Quinn asked.

"Until I have my money back and whoever did this is found," Gavin answered before quickly moving to another subject. "Honey, don't forget, you're meeting with my secretary and the other ladies at the hotel today about the society dinner and fund raiser."

"She'll have to get someone else. I'm staying here with Riley. I am trying to get an appointment for her to see a doctor. So far, no one can see her today or tomorrow."

"You've been harping about being involved with these events for a long time, and now you wanna back out? This is a big deal."

Quinn felt that Gavin had tunnel vision, only concentrating on what was best for the firm and rarely for their family. She felt like she was going to explode.

"Riley is going to be fine. She needs time. Ashley can keep an eye on her for a couple hours. Right Ash?"

"Gavin," said Quinn visibly angry. "She isn't fine! I cannot believe that you are walking around here acting like this is another regular day! Like nothing happened! She is not fine! Two men kidnapped her and they may have tried to bury her! How can none of this bother you?"

Gavin clinched his teeth. "I paid the money, Riley is safe."

Quinn eyed Gavin in disbelief. "She has been traumatized. What's more important than our children and their safety?" Quinn cried. "Riley has these crazy marks on her hand. We need to find out how she got them."

"You're kidding, she probably put them there with a permanent marker. Did you notice it before this happened?"

Quinn shook her head.

"It was probably there all along and you just never noticed, and I am thinking about their safety. If this gets out, that we paid a two-million-dollar ransom, we will be looking over our shoulders for the rest of our lives hoping and praying that we're not going to be targeted again and again. This is for the best. This is me protecting our family. And what would the board of directors think? This new deal could fall through because of this."

Quinn sighed, she felt once again defeated. "I can't believe what I'm hearing."

"Please," Gavin said. "Do the meeting. When you get back and you still think she needs to see a doctor, be my guest, but please do not mention the kidnapping or the ransom money. Ashley can call one of us if something happens, which I doubt it will."

Ashley glanced at Quinn who was displeased. "All right Gavin," she said with reluctance.

"I... I don't know," Quinn said.

"Go Quinn, I'll take good care of her."

"Fine," she said, firmly placing her cup on the counter and walking to her bedroom.

While Gavin was at work, Quinn was at the hotel planning the fundraiser, and for two hours, Riley sat in her bedroom on her bed with her legs crossed, staring into space. Every time Ashley checked on her, she found her in the same spot doing the same thing, just staring at nothing. Finally, as if someone called her, Riley crawled from her bed, stepped out of her room and peeked down the staircase. She could hear Ashley singing to music that was playing from the laundry room near the back of the house.

Riley walked down the stairs to the front door and peered through a window to see a man sitting in a black car across from the house, it was a security guard. She thought for a moment then crept down the hallway and into Gavin's den, careful not to make noise. She opened the French doors that led to a beautifully landscaped atrium and followed the stone path to the side of the house. She scaled the black rod iron fence with ease and hopped over. Riley gazed up at the fence, remembering two days ago when she tried to climb it and failed.

She glanced from one side to the other and saw no one. She inhaled a calming deep breath and sprinted away from the house. Riley's speed was remarkable, and she stayed out of sight by running down side streets and through bushes. She ran for ten miles and didn't stop running until she reached the outskirts of the city where a used luxury car lot sat. It was the type of dealer that helped those with no credit or bad credit, buy their dream car. She stood behind a street post and peeked around to see Stanley leaning against a late model black Panamera Porsche. His now shaved face was the picture of joy as a salesman approached him, wiped the hefty sticker price from the windshield and dropped a set of keys in one of Stanley's hands while shaking the other.

Stanley hopped in the car, sped out of the lot and down several streets until the paved roads disappeared, and became gravel. He came to a halt at a four-way stop sign. Since no other cars were in sight, Stanley preoccupied himself with the gadgets in the car, he was like a kid with a new toy.

The back door of the car swung open, startling him.

He looked in the back to see Riley hopping in, leaving the door open. Stanley's eyes widened in shock and anger.

"What the hell!"

Before he could think or say anything else, Riley leaned towards him and fixed her hands on both sides of his face, forcing him to see her shimmering and blood filled eyes. Her strength was fierce, he couldn't break free. She quickly dug her fingernail into his cheek, causing it to bleed. He began to whimper in pain, until she released him. She stepped out of the car and shut the door.

Stanley was incredibly calm and in a daze. He looked out of his side mirror at Riley who stood amused. He then gazed at himself in the rear-view mirror, studying the blood that ran down his face.

Under a spell, Stanley unfastened his seatbelt and without wavering, he slammed his foot on the gas pedal, pressing it as far as it would go. He reached a hundred miles per hour in no time, throwing dust from the dirt road. He veered off the road and headed at full speed towards a tree.

He didn't even close his eyes when the vehicle struck the tree, throwing him through the windshield, landing like a rag doll yards from the impact. Riley took a deep breath of air and exhaled with a grin as her eyes returned to normal. She calmly walked away.

Gavin's exhaustion was apparent by his unshaven face along with extra dark circles around his eyes. He stood in his office in front of his white board studying notes from an earlier meeting when he saw, through the glass wall, Jack approach. He immediately waved for him to enter.

Jack closed the door behind him and stood in front of Gavin.

"How are you holding up?" Jack asked.

Gavin sighed. "I'm fine. Quinn is a wreck and is wanting to go to the police, Dylan is frightened and Riley's in shock, understandably. My niece seems to be holding it together better than the rest."

Gavin walked to the other end of his enormous office to a small round conference table and sat. Jack followed.

"Most important thing is that Riley is home. Why don't you take some time off? Stay with your family until we can get a handle on things," Jack suggested.

"I don't want anything going wrong with this bid. If we win this, it sets us that much further from the competition. I need to stay on top of this and a couple of projects that we are about to finish."

"And you can stay on top of it from home."

Gavin sighed again. "You're probably right. It might make Quinn and the kids feel more safe."

"You've got the best working for you, let them do their job. Let me do my job. As soon as we get a lead, I will let you know. I have to head out of town for a couple days, but I have my partner, Devon, covering for me. Give him a call if you need anything," Jack said, standing. "You should go home Gavin. You look like shit."

Jack grinned and walked out of the office.

Quinn was not listening to Gavin's secretary, Irma, as she explained details of the upcoming fundraiser. They were seated at a large round table in the banquet room of one of the top luxury hotels in the city. The table was surrounded by mostly wives of Gavin's senior executive staff. Quinn's first thought was that she landed in the middle of a scene from the Stepford Wives. Everyone was perfectly dressed, not a hair out of place, nails professionally manicured and egos soaring. Quinn was uncomfortable, and even though she was the wife of the CEO, she wasn't given the same respect as the other women. Her insecurity showed on her face and she constantly picked at her fingernails and adjusted her clothes.

Quinn had many ideas for the fundraiser from her previous job as an assistant event planner, but she was apprehensive, and as she did with her marriage, she stayed quiet and waited for direction. Riley was all that was on her mind and she was stricken with the guilt of not being with her. Once again, she followed instructions from her husband, regardless of the cost.

When Irma stood, Quinn hoped that it was a sign that the meeting was coming to an end. It had already been two and a half hours. What more could they discuss? Quinn thought.

"Let's take a fifteen minute break," Irma said in a cheerful tone. "Then we can discuss how we can fit everything into the budget."

Quinn rolled her eyes and stood. She looked across the room and was happy to see her friend, Andi, standing at a table filled with snacks and beverages. Andi was a slightly taller light-skinned black woman in incredible shape. She showed off her toned arms wearing a sleeveless dress.

"I see you're as thrilled as I am to be here, my feet hurt," said Andi with a giggle as Quinn approached. "How are you and the kids? And when are you going to actually have lunch with me. Telling me next week over and over is getting old. We need to catch up."

"I'm sorry, things have been rather hectic," Quinn responded. "The kids are great, Riley is a bit under the weather. I was hoping that this meeting was wrapping up, but I guess not."

"I noticed across the table that you seem preoccupied. Having a kid sick can be draining. You're lucky Irma isn't making us take a test on what she covered," Andi jokingly stated.

"I'd fail for sure," Quinn replied with an uncomfortable disposition.

Andi filled a cup with hot water then slowly dipped a tea bag in. Quinn glanced at her watch.

"We've been friends for a long time, not that anyone can tell since we don't see each other anymore. I see it all over your face. Something is wrong, it can't just be that Riley is sick."

Quinn chuckled. "Is it that obvious?"

"Yes, it is. What's going on?"

Quinn looked away. "It's... It's just..."

"Is it Gavin? Are you thinking of the D word again?"

Quinn wanted to tell her friend the truth. She was alone but telling anyone what happened to Riley would go against Gavin's wishes and make matters worse.

"That thought left my head last year. Things are much better now."

Andi was not convinced. "I don't know how things are much better. You keep me shut out."

"What do you want me to do Andi?"

"It'd be great if you would think for yourself, it's always Gavin's way or nothing. You're not happy Quinn, I see it in your eyes."

Quinn bowed her head and then gazed at Andi with weary eyes. "Not today Andi, I can't discuss this today."

"Tell me what's going on?"

"Nothing, I'm fine." Quinn tried to sound convincing, but she knew Andi could see through her.

"You let Jackson, rest his soul, do the same thing but the difference is that he pushed you because you wouldn't push yourself to make decisions. Gavin tells you what to do only to benefit himself and he knows you will do it with no complaints. But the problem is still you. You have to start thinking for yourself and make you and the kids your priority."

"I know, I know," Quinn snapped. "And you wonder why I shut you out. I can't do this right now."

"Ladies, we need to get started again," said Irma from the other side of the room.

Quinn briskly walked away from Andi.

"I can't believe that lasted as long as it did," said Quinn frustrated as she stepped into the house from the front door. "I should have been home hours ago. Hey! Anybody home? Riley? Dylan?"

Ashley walked in from the kitchen. "What a long day Quinn, I can imagine how that went," she said as Gavin walked in behind Quinn. "And Gavin, I'm shocked to see you here."

"I'm finishing up work from home, this is going to be a long night," Gavin replied.

"I made dinner. I'll heat it up for you. The kids are upstairs," Ashley said as Dylan quietly entered the room. "Spoke too soon, here's one of them. Dylan will you run back up and get Riley?"

"How did she do?" Quinn asked.

"I checked on her a few times, she was staring at the wall all day. Hasn't said a peep. I am worried about her."

"She's not in her room," said Dylan.

"Yes she is," assured Ashley with a nervous chuckle.

"Check the rest of the house and out back, just to be sure," Gavin ordered.

"I haven't seen her since I got back from school," Dylan added.

Quinn became alarmed and shouted, "What?"

"Go look again!" Gavin hollered.

Dylan jogged back up the stairs while Ashley headed towards the back of the house to the patio doors.

"Ashley! What the hell were you doing?" Gavin shouted to her as she went outside. "You were supposed to keep an eye on her! There's no telling where she is!"

"We're calling the police! We can't go through this again!" Quinn cried. "Not again!"

As Gavin reluctantly walked to the kitchen to the telephone, Riley opened the front door and casually strolled in. Gavin sat the phone back on the counter.

"Riley, where were you?" Quinn asked, kneeling in front of her.

"I went for a walk," she replied, not fazed by what she had done earlier.

"Never again, young lady! You are never to go wandering around alone again. You hear me. You are going to cost me another two million dollars!" Gavin yelled.

"Screw your money Gavin!" she shouted, brushing past him.

Gavin reached for her, but Quinn stopped him. "Let her go, Gavin," she said in an exhausted tone.

He watched Riley run up the stairs, then glared at Quinn in disbelief. Quinn calmed herself with a deep breath, thinking of how she had never taken authority over Gavin as she just did. It surprised her more than him.

"Who the hell does she think she is? Where does she get off talking to me like that?" said Gavin in anger. "We didn't kidnap her!"

"This isn't about you! That little girl went through hell! Leave her alone!" Quinn screamed, knowing that it was time for her to take charge and not hide behind her thoughts of being shunned.

"So, what do you suggest? Do we let her go around acting out like this?"

"For now, yes."

Gavin raised his hands in surrender and said, "Fine. I've got some work to do."

"Of course you do," she said, watching him storm away.

CHAPTER SEVEN

The scene of Stanley's accident was gruesome. The Porsche's front end was still wrapped around the tree and his body, now covered with yellow tarp, laid where it landed after being thrown from the car. Police officers along with traffic investigators surrounded the area.

Detective Park Saire arrived behind a tow truck in a black unmarked police car. He stepped out and observed the small group of spectators before he made his way to the wreckage.

Park was part Peruvian, he was in his early thirties, and wore his shiny thick black hair short on the sides and fuller on top. His olive toned round face was clean-shaven but his five o'clock shadow seemed to frequently appear at three. He adjusted his leather jacket, making sure his hooded sweatshirt underneath laid perfectly at the waistline of his black jeans.

"Hey Park, welcome to the world of accidents and

suicides," said a police officer, walking to him then immediately feeling embarrassed. "I'm sorry man. That was a dumb thing to say. I didn't mean..."

"Suicides happen, right?"

"How are you doing? A bit of a shock to see you back this early."

"Life goes on," said Park with a sigh. "What brings me out here to a car wreck that you obviously think is suicide?"

The police officer gestured for Park to follow him to the back of the wrecked car and lifted the already partially opened trunk. Park peeked inside to see a duffel bag.

"What do we have here?" Park questioned with more interest.

The police officer gave him a pair of blue gloves. "That guy over there was thrown from this vehicle. Tire marks deep in the dirt about a hundred yards back, where he accelerated. No sign of attempting to stop, he just ran into the tree."

"Maybe he was distracted playing with his phone or the gadgets on this car. Porsche huh? Sweet ride," Park said, walking around to observe other angles of the car as he put on the gloves.

Park walked back to the trunk and opened the bag. His eyes widened when he saw hundred-dollar bills packed in ten thousand-dollar straps.

"Whoa," he said.

"This guy bought the car earlier today... for cash," the police officer commented. "We found the sales papers in the glove box."

"Gotta be about a million dollars here, minus what he paid for the car," Park concluded after thoroughly examining the stacks of money.

"Which is why we called you, his name is Stanley Cobson, works for a company called Rucker Architects."

"Where in the world did he get this kind of money and why is it in his trunk? What kind of work did he do?" Park asked, closing the bag and walking to the body.

"He was a janitor," said the police officer, following him.

Park raised an eyebrow. "We can assume that this money isn't his."

"And it's where we pass this ball to you. Here is his wallet," said the police officer, handing it to Park. "I'm going to see if they need help over there. You good?"

"Yep, all good. Have someone get that bag to evidence."

The police officer nodded and walked away while Park continued his stroll to the body. He knelt and lifted the tarp to see Stanley wide-eyed, probably from the sight of the tree ahead of him, Park thought.

He searched the dead man's pockets to confirm for himself that there was nothing else, then walked back to his car, hopped in and flipped through Stanley's wallet. There wasn't much except receipts from fast food restaurants and a few dollars along with his driver's license. Park studied it for a moment before placing it on the passenger seat. He started the car and drove away.

The next morning was brisk and chilly, but no matter what the weather, it was not going to stop Frank from making his trip down to the closest newsstand from his hotel to grab the latest newspaper. He wasn't good with computers and searching the Internet gave him a headache.

He needed to find someone who would listen to his story, someone that would believe his incredible words, someone that was living or about to live his nightmare. His explanation for walking the downtown streets was that it was where Lacey died and where he last saw the doll. He had one lead, which was downtown and the surrounding area, and he prayed that the truck that carried the doll didn't travel far.

Every morning, since losing his daughter, Frank would buy a newspaper, a cup of coffee and a muffin, and head back to his hotel suite. The suite was nothing grand, but it was functional with a small kitchenette, a separate bedroom, a living area and a place for dining. It was Frank's home until he found closure.

He made himself comfortable at a small round dining table and deciphered every word from every article that had to do with anyone dying from unnatural causes. Day after day, he found nothing, until that day.

He pushed the pile of old papers aside and began flipping through the pages of the paper that he just bought, carefully reading each headline until he came upon a short article with a headline that read 'Man Dies after Running Car into Tree'. He could feel his heart begin to race as he continued reading and jotting down notes on a pad of paper. It could be nothing, he thought, but he had to learn more.

"Gavin," said a young professionally dressed woman. She stood in the doorway of Gavin's office with Park behind her. "This is Detective Park Saire. He would like to speak with you."

Gavin stood from his desk, adjusted his suit jacket and approached the detective.

"Hello Detective," he greeted, extending his hand to him. "What can I do for you?"

Park grasped Gavin's hand and firmly shook.

"Why don't we sit over here," Gavin said, leading Park to the other end of his office to the small conference table.

Park admired the office. He examined the expensive furniture and tall green plants that were so well cared for that they appeared artificial. He was mostly impressed with the sixty-inch television mounted on the wall that aired a news channel with the volume muted.

"Sit, please," said Gavin, gesturing to a chair at the table.

They sat a couple chairs away from each other with Gavin feeling uneasy.

"Stanley Cobson," said Park. "Name sound familiar?"

"Excuse me?" Gavin responded in confusion.

"Do you know Stanley Cobson? Have you heard of him?"

Gavin thought for a moment then shook his head. "No. I don't believe I've heard of him. What's this about?"

"He is on your payroll as a janitor."

Gavin laughed. "A lot of employees are on my payroll, I can't say I know a third of them. Human resources and their managers handle the employees, maybe you should..."

"He's dead, ran his car into a tree yesterday. I thought maybe you would have heard."

"I'm sorry to hear and I didn't know. I'll have my assistant send condolences to his family. Now if that's all..."

"That's not all. It was an expensive car that he bought with cash. We also found a lot of money in a bag in his trunk," said Park.

"And how much is a lot?"

"I can't tell you that, unless you're missing some. I can't understand why someone with that kind of money would buy an expensive car, then run it into a tree and kill himself. We are calling it intentional for now, but it doesn't make sense."

"Oh?" Gavin questioned. "You have another theory?"

"I do. I wouldn't be doing my job if I didn't consider other scenarios and theories."

"And what's that?"

"That's my problem, I only have one. My theory is that maybe somehow he had something on someone like you and he was putting the squeeze on you," Park suggested.

Gavin became suspicious. "Squeeze? Where are you going with this?"

Park was blunt. "Was it your money?"

"No," he quickly answered.

"Do you make it a habit of hiring ex-convicts? Felons? Jail has been a revolving door for this guy for years. Seven months ago, he finished a year term for passing bad checks. Been with you for about six months."

Gavin reacted with a bite to his bottom lip thinking that even if he wanted to confess about the kidnapping and that it was probably his money, the death of the man changed everything, and now he had to stay silent.

"I believe in second chances," Gavin responded.

"You do background checks, that's good. Can't blame me for asking."

The men were in a stare down. Park felt that he had

struck a nerve with Gavin and his suspicions were high. Gavin was hiding something, but without any evidence, he knew he couldn't go any further with the interview. Gavin tried to hide his nerves and hoped Park didn't notice, but on the inside, he was terrified.

"Detective, I'm busy, if you have more questions about this man, I would appreciate it if you'd get to it. As I said, human resources can give you better answers about him."

Park stood, Gavin followed.

"Thank you for your time, please understand, we have to cover everything. We're waiting for the autopsy, but in the mean time, we need to find out where the money came from and how he got it. If he stole it maybe we can find out from whom and get their money back to them."

Gavin arched an eyebrow in interest as Park walked to the door and exited, leaving him standing in deep thought before he sat back at his desk. He lifted the receiver of his office phone and dialed a number. The call went to voice mail.

"Jack, I need you to call me the second you get back. I don't want to discuss this with anyone else," Gavin said, abruptly hanging up the phone, thinking about what he had learned from Park's visit.

Quinn carried a newspaper, the same paper that Frank read, under her arm. She walked into the kitchen and sat it on the island where Dylan and Ashley were eating cereal. Quinn never read the paper for the actual news, she was interested in the coupons that were packed inside the Sunday paper, any other day's paper wound up never read and placed in the recycle bin.

That particular day was different, she skimmed through pages until she saw a picture of a man and read the headline. It was Stanley's mug shot from his latest stay in jail. Alongside the picture was a photo of a crashed car showing his covered body on the ground. She became more interested as she read the story of the dead man and the unrevealed amount of money that was found in his car. Could it be the same man that kidnapped her daughter?

She ripped the article from the paper, folded it and put it in her jean pocket as Riley walked in wearing her pajamas.

"Riley, are you hungry? You haven't eaten anything in a couple days, unless you're sneaking food when no one is around," joked Quinn, pouring a cup of coffee.

"Stop asking me if I'm hungry. If I get hungry, I'll eat," Riley snapped.

Quinn sighed. She sat both the coffee pot and her cup next to the newspaper. She placed her hands over Riley's and rubbed them, taking note of the marks.

"You're starting to worry me with your lack of appetite. You haven't eaten a bite since you... since you were..." Quinn struggled to get the words out. "Why don't you hang out down here and watch one of your favorite shows."

"I'm going back to my room," she snapped again.

"I'll come up as soon as I can. I love you, Riley. We all do."

Riley faced both Dylan and Ashley with an evil eye before walking past them and up the stairs.

Dylan walked to Quinn. "Why is she being so mean?" he asked.

Quinn sat down and placed her hands on Dylan's

waist. "You both need to be patient. Give her time."

"Do you think they did something to her?" Ashley asked. "She's acting weird."

"Enough with your perceptions of her," Quinn ordered, annoyed.

"Did they hurt her?" Dylan asked.

"No, not physically. But she's been through a lot... mentally. We're lucky that she's still with us," said Quinn, giving Dylan a hug. "She needs time. She'll get back to her old self, you'll see. Now, you better get going before you're late."

"I forgot my book, be right back," Dylan said, heading up the stairs.

He reached the top of the stairs and saw that Riley's bedroom door was open. He stepped in.

"Riley, I just wanted to tell you that I hope you feel better soon," he said.

Riley sat in her bed leaning against the headboard staring at the television that wasn't on. Dylan chuckled. Riley scowled at him.

"Is that an imaginary show you're watching?"

Riley ignored him and continued in her mystified manner. Dylan gave a devilish grin and stepped in front of the television.

"Move out of my way Dylan," she said with no expression.

Dylan laughed. "Good grief Riley, why are you acting like a crazy person. Mom needs to take you to one of those quack doctors."

"Give me back my doll," she ordered.

"I don't have your doll," he responded.

"You hated her," she said in a bitter tone. "I know you took her. Give her back or get out."

Dylan became defensive. "What if I don't leave?"

Riley continued her trance-like stare. "Get out," she said again before getting angry. "Get out!"

"What's wrong with you?" he said, discouraged and confused at her actions. "I didn't take your stupid doll Riley!"

"Ostar!" she screamed, breathing heavy. "You can't stop it!"

Dylan dashed out of her room and back down the stairs forgetting his book.

"I gotta go, bye Mom!" he shouted, briskly moving past Quinn.

CHAPTER EIGHT

It was pitch black on the road Troy traveled in his SUV. A hard faced, blonde woman, Brandie, with a heavily made-up face, appearing to be in her late twenties, sat in the passenger seat. She was dressed in a skimpy dress that displayed a great deal of her legs.

At that moment, oblivious to the outside traffic, the woman began kissing the side of Troy's face, and rubbing his hair. Her cheap, red lipstick smeared his cheek.

"Tell me again how much you love me."

"Love won't mean a thing if you make me wreck the damn car. But hold the thought. We'll be at my place in a minute."

"Why can't we spend the night at a nice hotel? You said you're loaded," she whined. "Stanley is beyond annoying, I don't know if I can take another minute with him. I'd rather go back to my place."

Troy reached over to her and patted her knee.

"Can't stay in one place for long. I gotta wrap up a few things at my apartment and grab some important stuff from my desk. Won't be long before we're on our way to the airport and heading to some of the softest beds in the world. I promise. As for Stanley, he's harmless and soon, you'll never see him again."

"I like the sound of that."

As they came around the corner onto a street brightened by city lights, Troy noticed a police car and another car parked in front of his small rundown apartment complex. He immediately pulled to the curb and stopped.

"Whoa, what's this?" he questioned, continuing to stare through the windshield. "Cops at my building. Wonder what that's all about."

Troy climbed out, then stuck his head through the open window. "Hang tight. I'm gonna check this out."

Troy crept to the complex and beside the manager's office door. He could see a uniformed police officer and Park engaged in conversation with an older man who was the apartment manager. He crouched low, peeking through the partially opened door.

"Like I said, Stanley lives with his buddy Troy, but neither are home," said the manager. "Saw them both take off in a hurry a few nights ago, haven't been back since. I know that because rent is due."

"We have Troy as an emergency contact, but no phone. You wouldn't know how to reach him, would you?" the police officer asked.

"No, I don't. Troy has been a good tenant, up until now. He's never missed paying rent, always a few days early. What happened to Stanley?"

"He's dead. We are trying to find anyone that knew

him," the police officer answered.

"How well did you know Stanley?" Park asked.

"He was a nice guy. Stanley was a bit down on his luck. He had a job, but it didn't pay much, sounds like he was struggling financially. But he was always nice. Energetic guy, a talker, kinda like a big dreamer."

"Dreamer?" Park questioned. "How so?"

"He carried around a few pictures that he cut out of magazines. Expensive homes, cars, vacation spots... stuff only rich folks could have. He said that one day soon it would be his life. Not sure how he was going to do that unless he was going to rob a bank," the manager said jokingly. "What a shame that he's gone."

Troy quietly and slowly crept back to the SUV. He started the engine and began to drive.

"Change of plans," he said with no emotion. "Stanley somehow got himself dead. But don't sweat it, he's not our problem. I got the perfect place to stash the SUV and spend a couple of nights."

Brandie placed her hand on his shoulder and gave him a seductive grin.

It was past ten o'clock that night when Gavin walked in the house, he was distraught over the detective's visit and he found it difficult to focus on anything else. He was certain that the dead man was one of the men who took Riley and he couldn't help but to think that maybe Jack had done this. But, if he did, he was curious as to why he didn't take the money. He walked into the dim lit kitchen where Quinn was wiping down the counter.

"Hi Honey," Quinn said, surprised to see him. "It must be incredibly slow for you to be home before midnight."

She handed him the article she had torn from the newspaper about Stanley and he began to read.

"A detective paid me a visit about this guy today," he said, giving the paper back to her.

"It's one of the men that took Riley isn't it? It can't be a coincidence."

"He was one of our janitors, he had access to a lot in the building, including my office. Enough to come up with a plan to take Riley."

"And he had a bag of cash," Quinn added.

"Someone has some explaining to do as to how the hell an ex-con made it on my payroll," Gavin said noticeably agitated. "I don't think, or rather I hope this detective didn't notice, but when he told me this guy worked for my company and a bag of money was found, my eyes about fell out of my head."

"Maybe this is our chance to tell him what happened. What could it hurt?"

"Are you serious? The guy is dead. They'd try to connect us to his death, saying that we went out for revenge or something."

"Do you think he killed himself? I don't. He got away with a lot of money, why would he do that?"

Quinn sat on the couch, Gavin followed.

"Sounds like they aren't going to officially rule it a suicide until an autopsy is done. This detective doesn't seem convinced at all. If we don't say anything, then the only thing that ties him to us is the fact that he worked for my company."

Quinn became apprehensive to speak. "Did... Did you have anything to do with this? With that man's death?" Quinn nervously asked.

"No, but..." Gavin sighed and hesitated before continuing. "Jack may have."

"Oh my God," Quinn said in an exhausted tone. "You think Jack killed this guy and made it look like a suicide? It's a far cry from saying the only thing that ties us to this guy is that he worked for you."

"He's not going to bother us again. Be happy."

"The other one is still out there."

"Not for long if Jack has it his way," he said, pulling her to him and wrapping his arms around her. "We'll get through this."

She buried her head in Gavin's chest. "It's hard to believe he would kill himself but also hard to believe that Jack would do something like this."

It was morning, Riley tried to enter the bathroom that she shared with Dylan, from her bedroom, but it was locked. She stomped into the hallway to another door that led to the bathroom, it was locked too. She banged on it.

"Hurry up Dylan! It's not just yours!"

Ashley approached from her bedroom towards Riley.

"Riley, tell Dylan I'm outside and to be ready in fifteen minutes if he wants me to drop him off at school. I'll be outside pulling flowers that he needs for his biology class," she said, walking past her and down the stairs, ignoring the fact that Riley was mad.

The bathroom door swung open and Dylan stepped out to face Riley.

"Well it's about time," Riley said somewhat rude. "You're slow. You've always been slow."

"Wow Riley," Dylan responded, annoyed. "I get

priority since I actually go to school. Bathroom's all yours."

Riley swept past Dylan.

"If you don't stop being mean to me, I'm going to tell Mom and Dad," Dylan whined.

Riley faced him. "Go away! You're lucky Ostar protects my own blood."

Dylan laughed at Riley causing her to become angry. She tried to close the door, but Dylan put his foot in the doorway.

"Protect your own blood? What the heck does that mean?" Dylan snickered. "And who's Ostar? Your new boyfriend?"

Riley pulled the door open and reached for Dylan's face. Her fingers trembled as they touched his skin. She then violently threw him to the floor.

"Stop it Riley! What's wrong with you?"

Riley lunged at him, grabbing his arm and twisting it until she heard a snap. She then took hold of his face and looked into his stunned eyes for a moment before pushing him halfway down the stairs. When she heard Quinn and Gavin race up the stairs, she quickly stood as if she had done nothing wrong.

"What happened?" Quinn shouted, crouching to Dylan who was crying in pain.

"He wasn't watching where he was going and fell," she said with no concern.

Gavin knelt and sat Dylan up in his arms. "Hey buddy? What'd you do?"

"My arm!" he cried in pain. "It hurts!"

"I think you broke it big guy," Gavin said, lifting the boy in his arms. "Come on."

Quinn ran down the stairs to the front door and

opened it for Gavin. Riley made her way down the stairs to her mother and put her arms around her.

"I'm gonna take him to emergency, he's going to be fine," said Gavin. "I'll call you as soon as I can. And call my office, have them push my meetings to the end of the day."

Ashley, who was at the side of the garage uprooting flowers from the soil, saw the commotion and ran to them. "What happened?"

"He fell. He'll be fine," said Gavin as he got into the car.

Ashley glanced at Riley who was smiling and became concerned. After Gavin drove off, Quinn guided Riley inside, with Ashley close behind.

Riley was about to run up the stairs when Quinn stopped her. "Riley, how did this happen? You had to have seen something."

"We were kinda arguing about him taking forever in the bathroom. He was teasing me and calling me names. He was walking backwards and wouldn't listen when I tried to tell him he was going to fall. I tried to stop him. Serves him right."

Quinn was dumbfounded. "Why would you say that? He's your brother. You and Dylan have always gotten along well. You can't say things like that."

"Yes, I can," Riley said in an unnerving manner.

"That's enough Riley!" Quinn shouted. "I think you need to go up to your room and think hard about what you said. This isn't like you and it has to stop."

Riley walked away from Quinn, humming, not bothered by her mother's order.

An hour later, Ashley stepped into the family room where Quinn stood, studying photos that sat on the fireplace mantle. The pictures were in order with her favorite always in the center, which changed often. Her wedding photo had made its way to the end of the mantle.

"Any word on Dylan?" Ashley asked. "I thought you would be going to the hospital."

"No, Gavin called as soon as he got there. He didn't want me coddling."

Ashley rolled her eyes.

"They are putting him in a cast and then they'll be home."

Quinn placed her fingers on her temples and widened her eyes. "Riley has gone from zero to one hundred with her attitude, she's become a handful."

"Anything I can do?"

"You do too much already and honestly, I don't know what anyone can do," said Quinn. "Am I doing the right thing by listening to Gavin and keeping this all quiet?"

Ashley was silent for a moment as she thought to be careful with her words. "It's hard to say. As you know, when my uncle gets something in his head, there's no changing it. Sometimes his priorities can be messed up. You gotta listen to your gut."

After a few hours, Gavin arrived back at home with Dylan. His arm was wrapped in a cast from his fingers to his elbow.

"Don't move. I'll get Mom to make a place for you here," Gavin said, gently laying him on the couch.

Quinn scampered from another room to her son's side. "I'm sorry this happened."

"At least I get to skip school for a few days," he said, groggy from the medication.

"I'll get you a blanket and a pillow. You can watch TV until you fall asleep."

Gavin gave Quinn two small bottles of pills, and a slip of paper. "Here, these are samples, and this is the prescription, there's enough to get him through tomorrow. I need to get out of here."

"Wouldn't expect anything less," said Quinn, feeling exasperated as she watched him hurry out the front door.

"Where's Ashley?" Dylan asked.

"She's upstairs, I'll let her know you're here."

"And Riley?" he asked nervously.

"She's upstairs too. Wanna tell me what happened?"

"What did Riley say?" he fearfully asked.

"Never mind what Riley said. I want you to tell me what happened."

"I... I wasn't watching where I was going. I... I fell."

"Did she try to catch you?" Quinn questioned, somewhat suspicious.

"I don't remember. It happened kinda fast."

"It is such a horrible break for a fall down a half flight of stairs."

"Will you turn the TV on now? I'll fall asleep faster," he said, ignoring her comment.

"Sure," she said with concern.

Dylan slept comfortably throughout the rest of the day. Quinn checked on him often, sometimes sitting in a chair watching him. While she kept an eye on him, tending to his every need, Ashley helped with dinner. Quinn joined to prepare a plate for Dylan. Riley and Ashley were already at the kitchen island with plates in front of them. Ashley was scarfing her food while Riley sat quietly doing nothing. Her plate of food was untouched.

"Riley," said Ashley with a mouthful of food. "Did you see how Dylan broke his arm?"

"Good grief Ashley! You're not ten years old," Quinn

snapped. "Don't talk with your mouth full."

"He fell."

Ashley was embarrassed and swallowed what was left in her mouth, washing it down with water. "I thought I saw you smiling when your dad was putting him in the car."

"Oh, you mean Gavin?" Riley said in a bitter tone.

"That's enough!" ordered Quinn with a stern voice.

"I want to know what was so funny."

Riley began staring at the food on her plate but refused to eat.

"I doubt anyone was smiling," Quinn said, giving a plate of food and a glass of milk to Ashley. "Would you take this to Dylan?"

"Sure, and Riley, I'm sorry, I doubt you would ever be happy that Dylan was hurt," she said, walking away with the plate.

Quinn was beside herself with Riley's actions. "Sorry for what Ashley said, she didn't mean it."

"It's no big deal. She was being an ass. I wasn't smiling."

Quinn was surprised. "Why... Why did you say that?"

"Because that's what she is, she needs to be careful."

Quinn glanced at Riley's plate. "Eat your food before it gets cold."

"I don't want it."

"You haven't eaten in over two days. You have to eat."

Riley pushed the plate from her, hopped from the stool and skipped away.

That night, Quinn laid in her bed with her laptop

beside her when Gavin walked in.

"Hi," he cheerfully greeted.

Quinn was weary. "You're in a good mood," she said to him.

"I should be. We should be. We are on a very short list, I expect to close this billion-dollar deal within the next ninety days."

"I'm glad one of us had a good day."

"What? Dylan not doing well?" he asked, laying down beside her on the bed. "I peeked in on him and he was sound asleep."

"He's good," she said, laying her head on Gavin's chest. "It's Riley I'm worried about."

"You shouldn't worry," he said with no concern. "Until this blows over, I am going to try to work more from the house."

"I can't stop worrying. You've seen her 'I don't care' attitude, and you've heard the words that are coming out of her mouth. Today she said that Ashley was an ass. She's calling you by your name. She's all over the place! And all she does is sit in her room staring at nothing."

"She's on her way to becoming a teenager. They say mean things not to mention the crazy hormones. What happened to her was traumatic and it will be a while before the memory of this passes. Maybe it won't, I don't know, but don't try to blame Riley's inappropriate behavior on what happened to her."

"She won't even eat. I'm beyond worried."

Gavin was annoyed, he gently nudged Quinn from his chest and stood from the bed. "You know what? I don't want to deal with this. I'm bushed and I ache. I'll be in the hot tub," he said, walking out.

CHAPTER NINE

The next morning, Quinn walked into the family room as Dylan was awakening.

"Dylan? How do you feel?"

Dylan slowly opened his eyes and said, "Hungry."

"That's good. Ashley will bring you a snack. I'm going to run a few errands and then pick up your pain medicine before you run out of the samples."

Dylan became nervous. "Where's Riley?" he asked.

"Upstairs getting dressed. I talked to her teachers and she's going to stay home for a while longer," she said, kissing Dylan on his forehead. "Dad is working at the office for a few hours and then he'll be back. I'll be home soon."

Quinn wasn't gone long when Riley plopped on the floor in front of the couch near Dylan. Dylan guardedly watched her out of the corner of his eye when Ashley walked in carrying a plate of muffins.

"How about a snack? Nice and hot."

"All right! My favorite, thanks Ashley!" Dylan said with excitement as the telephone rang.

"You two share these," she said, walking away.

As soon as Ashley left the room, Riley grinned at Dylan and then at the food. She slid the plate closer to her. Dylan reached for it and Riley moved it further from him.

"There's enough for us to share," Dylan said with a crackling voice.

"No, not really."

She pulled him to the floor and began twisting his broken arm until the cast cracked.

"Ah! My arm!" he cried in pain.

Riley heard Ashley coming back in and released Dylan with a shove. Ashley saw Dylan on the floor crying in pain and quickly helped him back onto the couch, not noticing the damage to the cast. She was in disbelief that Riley wasn't doing anything to help Dylan.

"What are you doing Riley? What's wrong with you? Why did you do this?"

Riley lifted the plate and threw it at Ashley, barely missing her and shattering it against the wall.

"Take it all, bitch!" she yelled, running out of the room.

Riley ran outside to the backyard past the pool and hot tub and stopped at the end of the acre of land where there was a creek that actively flowed water. She stood for a moment watching the water as it moved down the creek before walking to the pool.

She sat down at the edge of the pool with her feet dangling in the water. Her reflection stared back at her until she splashed the water so that she could not see. She looked at the tattoo on her hand and caressed the two short bars that were faded. She covered her other hand over the marks when Ashley joined her at the side of the pool.

"Riley, what's going on? Why did you throw that plate?"

Riley bowed her head and continued playing in the water with her feet.

"Riley, please, I want to help you," said Ashley.

"I don't need help."

"You can talk to me. You know that, right? Do you want to talk about what happened to you? You can't keep it bottled up."

Riley drew her legs out of the water and sat at the edge with her legs crossed. "I'm good. Stop acting like you're my mom," she rudely said.

Ashley remained calm. "What about your friends? Why don't you invite a few of them over this evening? I can go and pick them up. You always have fun with them and maybe you'll start to feel like your old self again."

Riley started to uncontrollably laugh. "My old self? Why would I want to do that? I don't have any friends, they were never my friends."

Riley snapped her head straight and her eyes popped open as if she had remembered something important. She stood abruptly.

"I'm going back inside," she said, walking quickly to the back door, leaving Ashley puzzled.

Riley was eager to leave the house. She casually walked into Gavin's den and took the same escape route through the French doors and over the fence without being noticed by the bodyguard who sat in his car.

###

Troy and Brandie leaned against the front door of the cabin where Riley was held, kissing and mauling each other's upper and lower torsos.

Troy broke free of her. "Now that we've had a big morning feast, it's time to grab our stuff, pick up my IDs and get to the airport," he said.

"No argument from me. This is definitely not the place to bring a lady, but I'll let it slide," Brandie seductively said as she planted another kiss on his lips.

He pushed the door open and the two stumbled in to be welcomed by Riley who was in the middle of the room smiling and swaying her arms side to side.

"Hi Troy," she cheerfully greeted as if he was a good friend.

Troy's eyes widened in shock and he couldn't speak.

"Jail bait Troy?" Brandie asked with a chuckle.

Troy's mouth opened, but still, no words. Riley laughed, then lunged at him, knocking him on his back with her on top of him. Her eyes shimmered and the vessels in her eyes immediately blew as she firmly grabbed his face. She slit his skin with her fingernail, deep enough for blood to stream from his cheek. Troy tried to free himself from the girl's incredible grip but could not. Brandie shrieked and ran out of the shabby cabin's open door.

Riley released her grip and watched as Troy fought to get his bearings to sit up. He was calm as blood continued to flow from his wound. After a couple of deep breaths, he reached behind his back and pulled out his gun that was tucked in his jeans. In an instant, he put the gun under his chin and without fear, he pulled the trigger and fell motionless to the floor. Riley was dispassionate as her eyes went back to normal.

She spotted bags that were on the floor and began rummaging through them until she reached the one containing his half of the ransom money. She lifted it and swung the strap over her shoulder. Riley glanced around the dirty room before stepping over the body and quickly walking out.

Once outside, Riley checked all directions before running through the woods like a tiger stalking its prey, clinging tightly to the strap of the bag.

Brandie was exhausted from running aimlessly through the woods. Finally, she saw from a distance through the trees, a paved road. She was terrified and out of breath but continued running and pushing brush out of her way. She could hear someone quickly coming from behind her and began to run faster, tripping and pulling herself up several times. On her last fall, she looked behind her to see Riley standing and staring at her with a slight grin.

"What do you want?" she screamed at Riley with chills running through her body.

Brandie jumped to her feet and ran towards the street, continuing to check over her shoulder for the girl, but when she ran forward, she collided with her. Riley shoved Brandie with such force that she landed in the street, too late for an oncoming truck to stop. It struck her, throwing her out of her shoes and yards away, killing her instantly. Riley watched as the truck skidded to a stop. The driver exited and sprinted to the dead woman.

Feeling fully satisfied, Riley turned with the bag still strapped over her shoulder and calmly walked back through the woods.

###

Over an hour had passed since Riley's encounter with Troy and Brandie. Quinn continued to worry about Riley, not knowing what to do. She had been back for three days and continued to spend most of her time in her bedroom.

Quinn studied herself in the mirror in her bedroom. She then lifted the article of Stanley's death from her dresser and put it in her pocket.

Quinn wanted to give Riley as much space as she could but found herself standing outside her room knocking on the door.

"Riley, can I come in?"

There was no answer. Quinn tried opening the door but it was locked.

"Riley," Quinn called raising her voice. "Unlock the door, it's Mom."

Gavin was at home changing into his workout clothes when he heard Quinn and walked out of the bedroom wearing just his running pants.

"She's locked herself in," she said to Gavin.

Gavin tried to open the door with no success. He put his shoulder against it and forced it open to see Riley crawling in an open window beside her bed, with the bag still over her shoulder.

"Oh my God! Riley!" Quinn screamed in panic. "Gavin, grab her!"

Gavin ran to Riley, yanked her in and slammed the window shut. Riley was calm, Quinn was frightened and Gavin was furious.

"What the hell are you doing? Don't you know you could have fallen? What's the matter with you Riley?" Gavin scolded.

Riley dropped the bag at Gavin's feet. "Here's half of your damn money back," she said, glaring at him.

Riley walked to Quinn and stood beside her, watching as Gavin opened the bag. He was speechless as he sifted his hand through the stacks of bills.

"Where did you get this?" he asked in awe.

Quinn pulled the article from her pocket and sat Riley on her bed. Quinn and Gavin sat on opposite sides of her.

"Riley," Quinn softly said, holding the article in front of her. "Do you recognize this man?"

Riley rudely snatched the article from Quinn.

"Honey, do you recognize him, is he one of the men who took you?" she asked.

Riley crumbled the paper and threw it on the floor. She jumped off the bed, quickly walked to her desk, sat and began scribbling on paper, ignoring her parents.

"Riley. We're not done talking to you. Come back over here, please," said Gavin in a more calm and soft tone.

Riley became angry. "Oh yes, you're done. He deserved what he got and his friend too. We all know how much money means to you Gavin and now you have some of it back. You can stop your pathetic whining now. Thank me later."

Gavin caught hold of Riley's arm and yanked her from her chair. "What did you say? I don't care what has happened to you, don't you ever talk to me like that again!"

"Gavin, you're not making things any better. She's been through a lot," Quinn said. "Riley, what did you mean when you said, they got what they deserved? Where did you go? Where did you get this money? Did someone bring it to you?"

"Get out of my room," Riley ordered. "Get out now!"

"Okay, okay, we are going to leave. No more going out the window," Quinn scolded, standing and taking Gavin by his arm.

Gavin picked up the bag and went back to their bedroom with Quinn. He tossed the bag on the bed.

"How did she get this money?" Quinn questioned. "This is starting to scare me."

"Jack," he stated.

"Jack wouldn't give her a bag of cash and send her with it through her bedroom window. He wouldn't do any of this without telling us."

"It's the only explanation. He's on a job with another one of his clients, but I have a call in to him."

"And what about Riley? Now that you've seen more of her behavior, you gotta admit that something is off with her and she has been like this since the kidnapping."

Gavin sighed. "Let's not jump..."

"I'm done listening to you Gavin, this is our child! I 'will' be taking her to see a doctor tomorrow."

Gavin gave in, approached her and kissed her forehead. "Okay," he whispered.

Never had she made any demands from Gavin, but she knew if she didn't take a stand, Riley would never get the help she needed.

Gavin slipped on a sweatshirt. "Listen, I need to meet one of my project managers at another site, it's only thirty minutes from here, but we have to get this done by tomorrow morning. I won't be late."

Quinn replied with only a weak smile.

###

It had been weeks since Frank was able to sleep through the night. He could sleep two hours at the most before he would awaken, drenched in sweat and filled with heartache. It had been that way since he discovered what his daughter, Lacey, had become. Her face was eternally in his dreams, and nightmares of what she had done and how she ended her life, haunted him. The occurrences that led to Lacey's death played constantly in his head. He couldn't close his eyes without seeing that awful moment when she died.

He sat inside his car that was parked in front of a vacant downtown commercial building, listening intently to the radio when a broadcast aired.

"A twenty-six-year-old woman identified as Brandie Dent was struck and killed on Platt highway by a pickup truck earlier today. The driver of the truck stated that she appeared to have been thrown onto the street and he was unable to stop. Officials combed the nearby wooded area near where the accident occurred and found an abandoned cabin. Inside, police recovered Dent's belongings and discovered the body of a man identified as thirty-seven-year-old Troy Reynolds with a self-inflicted gunshot wound to his head. This past Monday, Reynold's friend and roommate, Stanley Cobson, died in what police initially concluded to be a suicide. Thirty minutes after Cobson's purchase of a vehicle, he collided into a tree and was ejected," said the broadcaster. "Police found an undisclosed amount of cash stashed in the trunk of the car and are now calling the apparent suicides and Dent's death, suspicious. Authorities are investigating possible motives along with where the money in the trunk came from."

Frank had new hope, there was finally a lead that gave

more information than he read in the paper. There were now two suicides and the assumption from the police was right, they were suspicious. He turned off the radio and circled an area on a map that laid on the passenger seat. He felt that he had enough information to believe that the doll with the pen was close. He started the car and drove away.

The sun was quick to fade before Frank found the cabin described by the news broadcaster. He sat for a moment staring at the police tape that surrounded the tiny shack. He felt his heart pound faster and faster as he walked to the cabin and ducked underneath the tape. He cautiously reached the door and tried to open it. It was locked. He peeked inside the window and then walked along the side of the cabin to the back. He wasn't clear on what he was searching for, but he knew he had to check it out.

He headed to an open field that resembled a junk yard. It was hard to tell if it was part of the same property or if it was a different lot. Old tires of various sizes were scattered about along with rims, unwanted appliances, rusted scraps of old metal and mounds of trash that were partially covered by overgrown grass and weeds. He walked a few feet beyond the trash and noticed an area where the ground was disturbed, and to his surprise, he saw the familiar tiny hand of a doll poking through the freshly moved dirt. He reached down and began pulling at the doll's hand through the earth until he had fully uncovered it. The doll that started it all had come full circle and back into his hands. He breathed a sigh of relief before frantically searching the doll. Even though he knew the pen wouldn't be with the doll, he was still stunned by the fact that it wasn't.

Frank continued to stare at the doll. "Where is it?" he

said in a panicky voice.

He was a step closer, closer than he ever dreamed, but until he could find the pen, his mission was far from over.

CHAPTER TEN

A few hours after Gavin left to meet with his project manager, he received an urgent message from Quinn that he was needed and had to return home. He was abrupt when he came in through the front door of the house where Quinn stood deeply worried.

"I got your message, what's wrong?"

"It's Dylan. His arm is hurting. Something is wrong and I th..."

"He broke the damn thing, Quinn. Have you been giving him his medicine? I have a lot going on at work and when I'm called away for..."

"Of course I have. If you'd let me finish a sentence. You've got to take him back to the doctor. I would have taken him myself, but he's in a lot of pain and I can't carry him."

"What do you mean?" Gavin asked, hurrying to Dylan who was on the couch moaning in pain.

"Bud, hey, let me see."

Gavin removed the blanket that was over Dylan, lifted his broken arm and examined the cast that was cracked.

"How in the world did you do that?"

"It hurts so bad!" Dylan cried.

Gavin lifted the boy from the couch and looked at Quinn, "I can't believe you didn't notice his cast! Get the door!" he ordered. "I'm taking him back to the hospital."

Quinn ran to the door and opened it, then ran out to Gavin's car, opening the back door. Gavin gently laid him down. He closed the door and jogged to the driver side.

Ashley heard the commotion and went outside. "What's happened? Is it Dylan?"

Quinn stood worried. She folded her arms and sighed. "Yes. Something happened to his cast, it's completely broken. I didn't notice. I should have noticed!"

Ashley was concerned as she watched Gavin drive away.

"Quinn," she said. "I am sorry that I didn't say something to you earlier."

"About what?"

"Riley had a meltdown. I gave her and Dylan a plate of muffins. The phone rang and I walked away to answer it. I didn't see what happened, but I heard this shriek from Dylan. I ran back in and he was on the floor crying. Riley stood there with this horrible evil look on her face."

"What? Did she hurt him? Do you think she did this?"

"I helped Dylan back to the couch and he said something about Riley not sharing the muffins. I didn't think to check his cast. I'm sorry. I was shocked at Riley's behavior. I told her to share and she threw the plate at me."

Quinn's eyes widened, she covered her mouth with her hand. "Oh my God, did she hit you?"

"No, but she was clearly angry," Ashley added. "I've never seen her in such a rage. Ever."

Quinn looked at her watch, with shaking hands. "Would you go and let her know that we need to get to her doctor's appointment. Thank God they found someone to see her this late."

Quinn patiently sat in the medical examination room with Riley who was not as tolerant. She sat on the examination table fidgeting with her fingers, continuously looking around the cold and sterile room.

"Riley, try to relax, I want to confirm that there's nothing we should worry about."

"Why would there be anything to worry about? I told you that I was fine. I can't believe you made me come."

"Well humor me then," Quinn said. "Do you want to read a magazine?"

"No," she pouted.

Quinn reached in her purse, held up a brand new iPhone, and dangled it in Riley's face.

"This arrived for you today."

Riley's face brightened as her mother gave her the phone.

"Thanks Mom!"

"I had all of your info moved to your new phone. You can use it whenever you want."

"This is great! I love it and it's upgraded!"

Quinn watched Riley behave like her normal self.

Maybe all she needed was time, she thought as a female doctor gently knocked and entered the room. She was in her mid-thirties and was casually dressed under her white coat. Riley continued to play on her phone.

"Hello, this must be Riley, I'm Doctor Flushing. We're sorry that your regular doctor wasn't available to see you. What's going on?" she asked as she sat on a stool in front of Riley.

"She's been a bit off," Quinn said.

"Off? How so?" asked Doctor Flushing as she stood and examined Riley's ears and eyes. "She doesn't have a fever and according to her vitals, everything is good."

"Can you do some blood work? She won't eat, in fact, she hasn't eaten since Sunday. Not a thing. She's gotten moody and it's out of character for her."

The doctor became more concerned. "Riley, how is your stomach, any aches?" she asked, getting no response from her. "Are you not hungry, or is something hurting you that is keeping you from eating?"

Riley finally sat her phone beside her on the table. "I'm not hungry. I feel fine," she said in a voice of innocence.

"Well you need to eat. Has anything out of the ordinary happened?"

"Like what?" Riley asked, becoming defensive.

"No," Quinn blurted. "Nothing unusual. I want to rule out any kind of bug she may have gotten, I'm concerned over her lack of appetite."

"I agree, it is concerning, especially for the amount of time she hasn't eaten. Usually signs of weakness and fatigue will have already shown. It does explain her moodiness that you speak of. It's odd that she's not showing any other signs, but I'll order blood work, a nurse will be in shortly and take it here in the exam room. I'll put it in as a rush to have the results back first thing in the morning. As soon as I get them and review, I'll give you a call Mrs. Rucker."

"Thank you," Quinn said with a sigh of relief.

"Nice meeting you Riley," said Doctor Flushing.

Riley picked up her phone and heard nothing else.

"I'm sorry," said Quinn, somewhat embarrassed.

"No problem, she's becoming a teenager. Need I say more?" she said jokingly as she exited.

"When can we go?" Riley asked, anxious to leave. She hopped off the table.

"Sit down, the nurse will be here in a minute. They are going to get some blood to confirm that there's nothing strange going on and then we'll head home. Maybe you want to stop for pizza and get your favorite toppings?"

"I want to go home, I don't want pizza," Riley responded, plopping in a chair beside her mom.

The nurse entered pushing a tray with a needle and vials. "Riley, this will take less than a minute. Can you show me your arm?"

Riley gave a bored sigh before extending her arm to the nurse who quickly drew three vials of blood and applied a dressing.

"There you go."

"About time," Riley said in an evil tone. "Now can we go?"

The nurse gave an amused look to both Riley and Quinn. "All set, have a nice day."

Frank stood inside the hall of his hotel room in front

of his door staring down at his cell phone in his hand. Although he had the doll, he was far from stopping the evil that had taken over someone else. He knew in his gut that the two recent suicides were the path to him finding the person that had the pen. He had to try.

Frank inserted his key into the door and before he opened it, he began to think more about the doll that he held under his arm. He was tired, but sitting in his room wasn't going to bring him closer to what he had to find and time was running out. He removed the key from the door, pulled out his phone and dialed a number. Now that he had the doll and considering where he found it, he hoped for a better chance to locate the person that had it last and find the pen.

"I need to speak to whoever is investigating the deaths of Troy Reynolds and Stanley Cobson," he said into his phone. "Wait, did you say Park Saire?... I need to speak to him. I have information... No, I won't talk to anyone else... Sheppard Hospital?... Thank you."

His face brightened as he stuck his hotel key back in his pocket and walked nimbly down the hall and out the door.

Doctor Brian Hogue was a tall and lean man in his mid-forties, styling a short salt and pepper haircut. He casually walked into the emergency waiting room to greet Gavin who was on his phone talking business. He ended the call when the doctor approached.

"Gavin, we gave Dylan a new cast," he said. "He's fractured his arm above the original break."

"How could that happen?"

"That's what I was about to ask you and honestly, I should have questioned the first break."

"Excuse me," Gavin said, becoming more concerned. "What are you talking about?"

"I don't believe he fell down the stairs in the manner he said."

"You're calling him a liar?"

"Someone twisted that boy's arm. It's the only way that cast could have broken the way that it did. I am feeling the same with the original fracture."

"Riley and Dylan were the only two there, they say the same thing, he lost his footing and fell. They're both good kids. Maybe he caught it in the rail and twisted it and that caused the first break. Could this second one have happened by a fall from the couch?"

"Highly unlikely, but that's my opinion. We should ask him again what happened," suggested Doctor Hogue.

Gavin followed the doctor down the hallway and behind a curtain where Dylan laid on a narrow emergency room bed.

"How ya doing buddy?" Gavin asked, rubbing his hand across Dylan's head.

Dylan innocently looked at Gavin, then at the doctor.

"Dylan, tell us again what happened to your arm," Doctor Hogue instructed. "Your fall isn't consistent with the break you have. Can you tell us how this really happened?"

Dylan watched his dad and the doctor as they waited for his response.

"Dylan," said Gavin, leaning in to him. "Did you fall down the stairs the first time? Or did something else happen?"

"You won't believe me," Dylan softly said in a defeated tone.

"All we want is for you to tell us the truth. Please," Gavin begged.

Both men stared at him, anxious for him to speak which made Dylan more reluctant to say anything. He inhaled and deeply exhaled.

"Riley twisted my arm, I didn't fall at all. She did it," he admitted. "She is still mad at me because she thinks that I took her doll but I didn't."

Gavin and the doctor glanced suspiciously at one another.

"And what happened today?" Gavin asked.

"She was supposed to share the muffins that Ashley gave us and when I tried to get one, she twisted it again."

"But how?" Gavin questioned in confusion.

"I told you that you wouldn't believe me. It's what happened. She's not the same. Ever since she was kid..."

"Dylan, thank you for telling us," interrupted Gavin.

"How is Riley not the same?" Doctor Hogue asked, baffled as to why Gavin interrupted Dylan.

"She's mean to me. We joke around a lot but she's never gotten this mad at me, ever. She's awful."

As Dylan explained to the doctor and Gavin, Frank listened near the curtain.

"Riley's been having a rough time at school with her friends," said Gavin, wiping his forehead. "You know how girls can be. She brings it home and takes it out on everyone else."

Dylan bowed his head in disbelief that his dad was lying in front of him. He wished he could tell someone that Riley was kidnapped and that she wasn't the same. He missed her.

"That's not an excuse to literally break the little guy's arm... twice," said Doctor Hogue. "He can go home as soon as the nurse finishes the papers. Have him continue the medicine I prescribed for the pain. I want to see him next week Tuesday, call my office and make an appointment. Gavin, may I speak with you?"

"Dylan, bud, I'll be back. Stay put," said Gavin.

As Doctor Hogue opened the curtain, Frank quickly backed around a corner of the corridor, disappearing from sight. He peeked the other way down the hall and saw a man strolling to Gavin and the doctor, it was Park.

"Sorry I'm late, Doctor. I made it as soon as I could," said Park.

"Not a problem Park. This is Gavin Rucker, the man I told you about," said Doctor Hogue. "Gavin, I had no choice but to…"

"We've met," said Park.

"Yes, we have. What are you doing here?" Gavin suspiciously asked. "What's going on?"

Gavin's eyes shifted from Park back to Doctor Hogue, reflecting wonder. Park extended his hand to Gavin who had no interest in shaking.

"Doctor Hogue called me. He's expressed some concern about your son."

Gavin became defensive. "Oh? You couldn't consult with me first? What concerns are you talking about?"

"Park, I'm afraid I may have wasted your time," said Doctor Hogue. "We spoke with Dylan again and he confessed that his sister did this to him."

Park raised his brows. "His sister broke his arm, twice? How old is she?"

"Twelve," Gavin replied, aggravated.

"Wow, she must be strong to be able to do that," Park responded in astonishment.

"What are you getting at?" Gavin suspiciously asked.

"Apparently nothing. Doctor, if you don't need me

then I'll be on my way."

"Wait a minute!" Gavin snapped. "You thought me or my wife did this, so you call the police?"

"Gavin look, it is protocol," Doctor Hogue tried to explain.

"Calm down Mr. Rucker, he was doing his job and you should consider yourself lucky that he called me and not social services," Park scolded. "Now I suggest that you have a talk with your daughter. Sibling rivalry can be tough especially when it gets to this. You have your hands full to keep this from happening again. Next time you, or your daughter for that matter, may not get off this easy."

"Not a problem," Gavin said in a displeased manner, walking back to Dylan.

Doctor Hogue and Park watched as Gavin disappeared behind Dylan's curtain. Once he had Dylan up and ready, they walked from behind the curtain.

"Thank you both," Gavin grumbled as he slowly walked past the doctor and Park, guiding Dylan.

"Are you satisfied with the kid's story? Hell of a break for a twelve-year-old girl to do."

"I'm not sure. I've known those kids since they were babies, I even went to Gavin and his wife Quinn's wedding. They aren't the kind of people that would hurt their kids. Though we're never sure of what goes on behind closed doors, I can't see either of them harming the children. Sorry I had you come out for what is probably nothing. As long as they nip this now," said Doctor Hogue. "And how are you doing? I am surprised that you've gone back to work. It seems too soon for you to be back. Not a day passes where she isn't on my mind."

"Thanks Brian. Work is what I need. My parents are

back in Chicago and there's nothing left to occupy my time."

"Take it easy. Anything you need, a night out, joining my family for a barbecue, poker, whatever."

"I may take you up on all of those," Park replied, pulling a pen and notepad from his pocket. "Even though this is a false alarm, I would like to make a record of this. I need the Rucker's address."

Doctor Hogue raised his clipboard carrying a chart. "45287 West Oakleigh Drive," he said.

Frank abruptly hurried around the corner to the men. "The boy! He is a victim!" he exclaimed like a mad man.

"What?" asked Park who was startled by the man.

"Are you Detective Saire?" Frank asked.

"I am. And you are?"

"My name is Frank Lighton," he said politely tipping his cap. "The boy is right. His sister has changed and she will continue until she completes her quest."

"Oh?" questioned Park in disbelief and widening his eyes to the doctor with a thought that the man was crazy.

"There's not much time, you have to trust me. Those two men, the one from the car and the other in the cabin, they weren't suicides. Well they were suicides, but someone made them do it and those men are somehow connected to that boy's sister."

"Mr. Lighton. Is there someone I can call, a family member, a friend or anyone who can come and get you?" asked Doctor Hogue.

Park rolled his eyes.

Frank's efforts remained frantic. "Please, don't patronize me. I know what I'm talking about. My daughter couldn't be saved and neither can his. She's no longer their daughter, but there is still time to try to save others," he said.

Park was bothered by the man. "Couldn't be saved? And what happened to your daughter?" Park questioned.

Frank was eager. "She's dead now. But ... But... Please, listen. Danger comes from that girl!"

Park slapped his hand on Frank's shoulder and took him by his jacket.

"Come on, move on before you wind up sleeping in a cell."

"Ask her about the doll and if she has the pen!"

"I'll see you later Doc. Come on Frank."

Park escorted Frank who was very reluctant, to the exit. When they reached the outdoors, Park released him with a shove.

"Go on! This is your last warning."

Frank refused to walk away. "You must listen to me. Please! Those two men, do you know why they killed themselves?"

Park started walking through the parking lot, Frank followed him.

"We are investigating that," said Park as he continued to walk. Frank struggled to keep pace with him. "Stay out of it, we have it handled."

"No, you are far from having this handled. Tell you what," said Frank, pulling the doll from his pocket. "This is the doll that the boy spoke of. If his sister recognizes it, then she has come in contact with both of those men that supposedly killed themselves."

Park slowed his stride to see what Frank was carrying, then sighed. "Where did you find it?"

"If this belongs to the girl," Frank said, ignoring Park's question and offering him the doll along with a slip of paper. "You must give me the chance to explain all of what has happened and what is to come."

Park took the doll and the paper from the man.

"Please, you can reach me at that number," said Frank, stepping back. "There isn't much time, take the doll to the boy's house, then you will begin to realize that I'm not crazy," he said before slowly walking out of sight.

Dylan sat quietly in the front passenger seat of the car. Gavin rubbed his chin in deep thought as he drove.

"You don't believe me, do you?" Dylan asked.

"Hard to swallow. But we'll all sit down and get this figured out."

"She's not my sister. I'm scared of her and I don't want to go home," he whined.

As they stopped at a red light, Gavin watched his son who caressed his broken arm that was snug in a sling. Dylan was never afraid of anything, Gavin thought. But there he sat, shivering and on edge.

Gavin sighed. "Your buddy Aaron's mom called us when she heard that you broke your arm, she offered to help out with you. With her being a nurse at the hospital, I think we should take her up on it and see if you can stay there tonight, maybe for a couple nights."

CHAPTER ELEVEN

Park stood behind the manager of the apartment complex where Troy and Stanley lived, waiting for him to unlock the door to their unit.

"Quite the coincidence that Troy was found dead the same week his buddy died," said the manager, fiddling with the keys. "I'm not one to get all caught up in the news, but after Stanley's death, curiosity got the best of me so I turned on the news to learn more, then I hear that Troy has passed away too. How crazy is that? You think they both got tired of the struggles they faced once they got out of jail? Can never tell. Now I gotta get this place cleared out. I need the rent."

Park rolled his eyes as the manager finally opened the door and swung it open, allowing Park to walk in ahead of him. The unit was nearly bare. There was an old recliner and matching sofa around a small wooden coffee table, and two folding chairs that sat in the kitchen with a card table.

"When you're done, stop by the office and I will lock it up," said the manager as he walked out.

Park put rubber gloves on his hands and sat at a desk that was in the dining area. He searched a drawer that contained a few pens, pencils and blank note pads. The only thing that appeared of interest was a small manila envelope. He lifted it and dumped out several pieces of paper of different sizes with notes written on them. Park carefully read each one, discovering nothing of importance until he reached a folded sheet of paper with information that made his eyes widen. He yanked a plastic evidence bag from his pocket and dropped the paper inside.

It was night. Gavin walked into the house from the garage door that led into the kitchen. Dylan was safely at his friend's house and everyone except Quinn was asleep. She was sitting on the sofa with a soft light illuminating the family room. He joined her.

"How is he?" Quinn asked.

"Relieved," said Gavin with a sigh. "Thanks for agreeing to let him stay with Aaron. I'd never seen him scared to come home."

"He really said that Riley hurt him?"

Gavin nodded.

"Ashley told me that Riley flipped out on her and Dylan."

"Over muffins is what Dylan said," added Gavin.

"Yes, but I feel like there is more to it. I believe him, I believe that Riley hurt him. Ashley said that when she heard Dylan scream and found him on the floor, Riley wasn't doing anything but standing there watching," she whispered. "She also threw the plate at Ashley. We need to find out what's going on with her. Why does she want to hurt her brother?"

"He said she thinks he took that doll she found. Good riddance to it however it got out of the house. But Dylan is terrified of her. How did the doctor appointment go?" Gavin asked.

"We will have blood results in the morning. If anything, it should show low blood sugar from lack of food."

"Are you sure she hasn't eaten anything? It's been days."

"I don't know anymore," she said. "What about that weird tattoo on her hand and how did she get it? The changes in her behavior and what she did to Dylan, it all makes me believe that something happened to her that day when she was taken."

"You're talking like she's possessed," he said with a chuckle.

"Can you survive five days without food? I haven't even seen her take a sip of water."

"No, I can't, and neither can Riley. She's obviously raiding the fridge. She's playing you."

"I don't think..."

"Enough!" he yelled, frightening Quinn. He immediately calmed down. "I'm sorry, as soon as I hear from Jack it'll at least clear the mystery of this Stanley guy and the duffel bag."

They heard a faint knock on the front door. Quinn stood behind Gavin, curious to know who was visiting at that hour. It was Park. Gavin opened the door.

"Detective," Gavin greeted in an unwelcome tone. "What can we do for you at this hour?"

"My apologies for coming this late, but I wanted to take a chance that maybe your daughter Riley was still awake, and I'd also like to speak with you two."

"Even if she was awake, I wouldn't let you near her," said Gavin. "I'm tired of you popping up."

"I'm Quinn Rucker, Gavin's wife. I assume you are the detective that visited my husband at his office."

"Yes, I'm Detective Park Saire."

"Why do you want to see Riley?" Quinn asked.

Gavin was irritated at Quinn and frowned at her.

Park pulled the doll from his jacket pocket. "Is this hers?"

"Where did you get that?" Quinn questioned, snatching the doll from him.

"It is your daughter's," Park confirmed.

"Wait, wait," Gavin snapped, "What's going on?"

"Please Detective," said Quinn. "Come in, this isn't something we should be discussing at our doorstep."

Quinn nudged Gavin to the side to allow Park to enter. She closed the door then led him to a recliner and gestured for him to sit. She and Gavin sat close together on the sofa.

"What's going on? Where did you get this doll?" Quinn questioned.

Park eyeballed Gavin and rubbed his chin before speaking. "Gavin," he said, leaning closer to him. "I think you lied to me."

Neither Gavin nor Quinn uttered a word.

"Stanley Cobson, the man we talked about in your office, his roommate was a man by the name of Troy Reynolds. Reynolds also committed suicide. You may have heard about it on the news."

"Yeah, so," Gavin replied.

Quinn and Gavin listened intently to every word Park said, both were anxious as well as suspicious of what Park knew.

"Obviously this is suspicious. Both were criminals, both served time at the same facility," he said. "What caught my eye is what I found in Troy's apartment."

Park raised the evidence bag that held the sheet of paper that he found in Troy's desk. Gavin had a lump in his throat along with a sick feeling in his stomach.

"This seems to be a 'to do' list on snatching your little girl. Troy's job was to snag Riley and negotiate the ransom. Stanley's big task from this was to get as much information on you, since he had access to your office. My question to you is, why would you keep it a secret? These two men kidnapped your daughter and the money in Cobson's trunk was what you paid as ransom or at least half. It says two million on this sheet."

Gavin stood and stepped away. He swallowed hard before he spoke. "They said no cops or she would be dead."

"We did what they said and we got her back," Quinn added.

"Did you know that Stanley Cobson was one of the men that kidnapped Riley?"

"I figured he was, after your visit to my office."

"Could it have been before my visit?" Park suspiciously asked, not taking his eyes from Gavin.

"Why don't you come out and say what you've come to say, I'm not playing your game."

"Did you figure out who did this to your daughter and decide to take matters into your own hands? Did you have anything to do with this guy's death? Revenge maybe? I can't understand why you would leave the money in the trunk."

"Exactly," Gavin growled. "I wouldn't have."

"I'm curious to know why there wasn't any money found with Reynold's body."

Quinn stood, approached Gavin and rubbed his shoulder. "Calm down. Detective, when we heard of his death and that money was found in his trunk, plus the fact that he worked for Gavin's firm, we couldn't help but assume that he was one of them. But we had nothing to do with his death. If we did, trust me, we would have taken the money."

"Then we hear about this guy, Troy Reynolds, being found dead in a cabin and that he was Stanley's roommate," Gavin added. "We knew they were the ones. We surely weren't going to the police at that point. They would try to tie these deaths to us. It's what you're thinking. I'm not going to lie, I'm glad they are gone but we didn't kill them. We paid the two million in ransom, but I can't tell you what happened to the other half."

Gavin returned back to the couch and sat.

"The doll," said Quinn. "How did you know it belonged to Riley?"

"As I was leaving the hospital, this older gentleman comes to me and tells me that your family is in danger. He basically said that Riley is the root of it all and that she's no longer your daughter. Then he gives me this doll and says that if it's hers, I owe him the chance to explain what this is all about."

"Well call him!" Quinn exclaimed, immediately and anxiously sitting beside Gavin. "She found the doll the same day she was kidnapped. And now, something is wrong with her. If he can explain this, then we have to hear him out."

"Explain what Quinn?" Gavin asked in a bitter tone.

"Her behavior! Her demeanor! Her attitude! She has changed since they let her go. I don't know if what those kidnappers did to her is making her crazy like this or if it's that doll! They both came into our lives on the same day!"

"Detective, ignore my wife, sometimes her imagination can get the better of her. What can this guy possibly say about that damn stupid doll other than to confirm where those assholes probably held her? Did you ever think that maybe he's a fraud? Maybe this guy had something to do with Riley's kidnapping," Gavin said.

Quinn became frustrated, but unlike any other time when Gavin talked over her, she wasn't going to be silenced.

"Oh please, Gavin, why on earth would he go through tracking down this detective and being insistent with the doll?"

"If you're even thinking that this disgusting doll is more than a doll, leave me out of it."

Quinn shook her head and sighed.

"Detective, we swear to you that we had nothing to do with their deaths. I don't think the man gave you this doll to show you that those awful men kidnapped Riley," said Quinn. "There's more to it, I know it. He said Riley is no longer our child, right?"

Park nodded.

"I want to know what he meant. He said that if the doll is Riley's then you owe him a chance to explain."

Park sighed. "We can talk to him."

"Please Detective," Quinn pleaded. "Contact him. I need to know what he knows."

"We'll find somewhere to meet him first thing in the morning."

"And how do you know he's not part of all of this?" Gavin asked. "This isn't one of your favorite horror shows."

Quinn gave Gavin a defensive glare.

"Your wife is right, this man is more concerned about that doll and protecting your family."

Gavin wiped his hand across his face. He was frustrated with the discussion. "I don't care how he got the doll. The men that did this are dead, the end," he said, getting up and strolling away.

CHAPTER TWELVE

The restaurant where Frank waited was located a few miles from the Rucker's house. It was less busy on weekday mornings, but at any other time, it was a popular spot for families that lived in the area. The sun had barely risen when it opened, and Frank was the first to step in. He found a booth at the far end of the diner and sat. He could barely sit still, not even pushing and rubbing his aching thigh could stop his leg from trembling. He began fidgeting with his fingers when he finally saw Quinn and Park enter. Frank stood from the booth and waved for them to join him.

"Frank," greeted Park. "This is Quinn, Riley's mother. Quinn, this is Frank, he found the doll."

Frank shook her hand and gestured for them both to sit. Park and Quinn sat together on one side across from Frank.

"The doll, was I correct in that it belonged to your girl?" Frank asked. "Wouldn't be sitting here with you now, had it not been, I assume."

"What do you know, how did you get the doll?" Park asked.

Frank sighed. "Where to begin. I've been hoping for the day to tell this story and now I stumble at where to start."

"Start at where you found the doll," Park suggested.

"Right, yes, perfect," said Frank. "I have been searching for that doll, particularly what the doll had for about three weeks. I've been researching every case in this area that had to do with suicide. I heard on the news and read in papers about two men that committed suicide. One of the men was found dead in a cabin. That is where I found the doll. It was partially buried in an area behind it."

"He was one of the men that kidnapped Riley. When she came home, she was covered in a lot of dirt, possibly from where you found the doll," said Quinn. "I think they tried to bury her. Why would they do that only to send her home?"

"Because they thought she was dead, like my daughter," Frank blurted.

"What?" Quinn was wide-eyed.

"Come on Frank, don't you think you've taken this a bit far?" Park questioned.

"I needed to see for myself, I hoped to find something and I did. I was standing there with this doll that carried something that was meant for me. It's like a contagious deadly disease."

Frank became frustrated with himself.

"Oh dear," he said, taking off his baseball cap and rubbing his hand over his perspiring forehead and across his balding head. "I'm not doing well at explaining. Let me go further back, to my beginning."

It was the middle of the night when Frank began his drive that led him two hours into what seemed like the middle of nowhere. He was in the woods where the trees stood tall and were surrounded by darkness. He shut the engine off and stared through the windshield up to the clear skies. He could see every star.

Frank glanced to his glove compartment and then back to the sky. After a few moments of being drawn to the glove box, he opened it and eased out a pistol. He examined it for a moment before sobbing.

"I can't do it! I want to do it, but I can't die this way! They will get nothing! What do I do?"

Frank began beating his hand against the steering wheel. "They're better off without me! I've failed them! I don't know what to do!"

Frank continued to sob until he heard a knock on his window. It was dark and he couldn't see clearly. He rolled the window half way down.

"What do you want?" Frank guardedly asked the man who wore a dark long coat with a hood over his head. He had on dark gloves with the tips cut out revealing his olive creped skin.

"I want to help you," said the man who stood around six feet. His voice was deep and sounded as if he were speaking under water.

"Who are you? I don't know you."

"You're a man at the end. I see that, I've seen it."

"What? You've been watching me? How?"

"You come out here often to do what you don't seem to have the courage to do. Come out, talk to me. I want to offer you a chance, a way out for your family."

"Unless you're planning on killing me to allow my family to collect the insurance, I don't want to hear what you're offering."

"What would you say if I told you that I can save your family and all you'd have to do is one favor for me? Come out. Let's talk."

Frank was hesitant and thought for a moment. Feeling as if he had nothing to lose, he stepped out and examined what he could of the man who wore a tight black shirt and black pants underneath his coat that outlined a thin and fit physique. Frank observed the mysterious man's blood red eyes and pupils that shimmered on and off.

"I want your soul," was all the eerie man said.

Frank leaned against his car and laughed, thinking the man was crazy. "Who the hell are you? What's your name?"

"Ostar. My name is Ostar. I am the survivor and leader of my realm, and with your help, it will resurrect. I am about to give you magic that is yours to use against anyone but your own bloodline."

"Bloodline?" Frank asked confused.

Ostar ignored Frank and continued, "Once the magic is over for you, all I ask is for you to pass it to someone else who is down on their luck and trying to find a way out. Once a sin is now an act of giving. You'll be the beginning, a new genesis for my kingdom."

"Wow, magic," said Frank with a bit of humor. "What kind of magic?"

Ostar reached into his coat pocket and pulled out a small doll made of beige fabric and tossed it to Frank.

"A doll?"

"What is special is what it carries. Take this and the mistakes you've made will be as if they never happened. Your wife and your daughter will live happily ever after."

Frank was confused, he gave a nervous chuckle.

"Go home, the doll will help you. You will know when it's time and you will know what to do."

"What kind of nonsense is this?"

"If you want to end the suffering and financial bleeding that

you've caused, you'll take the doll and what it possesses. Take it and a half million dollars will appear in your bank account, enough to pay off your gambling debts with enough left to free your family."

The sound of financial freedom piqued his interest. "Tell me, how exactly does this work?" he questioned.

"It's quite simple, your forfeited soul will find new life with me, in my kingdom. Every one hundred years my realm must be revived. Your soul will begin the journey to restore life to my world and before you give it to me, all you need to do is pass the doll to someone else."

Frank was still in disbelief, but he was curious. "Where are you from?"

Ostar removed his hood revealing his long shiny black straight hair that was as thick as straw draped over his shoulders and down to his waist. His pupils that centered the blown blood vessels in his eyes continued to shimmer. The skin on his face was like worn crackling leather. His lips were dry and small traces of blood seeped through the creases as he spoke.

"I come from Nesuree, a world far from yours. Mine is dying and human sacrifice is how I can save it. Twenty souls, it is little to ask. This is my one chance, and when sent to me through this magic, the blood of Ostar, my world will once again awaken."

"And if I don't agree to this?"

"I will leave you to what you were planning. You will kill yourself and leave your wife and that beautiful daughter in more debt than when you were alive. Why not die with my magic knowing you have helped your wife and your child?"

"And if I agree and then change my mind?"

Ostar became angry and in less than a second, he charged to Frank, almost touching his face.

"There's no going back! Your blood isn't pure enough to stop this! You can't stop this!" Ostar roared before becoming calm.

Ostar stepped away from Frank and scanned him with his eyes.

"Before you decide, why don't you check your bank account? Get a glimpse of what you can do for your family."

"Why? There's no reception out here," Frank said as Ostar continued to stare at him.

Frank checked his cell phone that he had taken from his pocket and saw that he did indeed have reception.

"That's odd," he said as he logged into his account. His eyes widened in shock at the sight of a half million-dollar balance in his account.

"I can make it disappear as quickly as it appeared."

Frank contemplated for a moment before saying, *"Okay."*

Ostar gave a devious grin and said, *"Take this doll and go home."*

Frank drove home with the doll that sat face down in the passenger seat. He kept wondering if he would wake from this incredibly crazy dream, and if it wasn't a dream, he worried how the magic would actually work.

He was exhausted when he finally arrived in his driveway. He got out of his car, leaving the doll behind. It was past two o'clock in the morning, the house was dark and quiet. All he wanted was to drop in his bed and sleep, which is exactly what he did.

The next day, Frank was awakened by the bright sun that filtered in through the blinds and sprang from his bed. It was noon and his wife had long ago left for work. He looked at the clock and couldn't remember the last time he slept sound and for so long. He strolled into the kitchen and peeked out the window at the bright sun.

Panic set in the second he saw that his car was gone. He looked at the calendar on the refrigerator, it was the day for the car to go to the shop for service. His daughter, Lacey, must have taken it, he thought.

Frank paced the kitchen floor for an hour waiting for Lacey to return. Finally, he heard the car pull into the driveway. He came out of the house to see Lacey exiting with the doll in her hand.

"Hey Dad, Mom asked me to take the car down to get the oil changed. She said she didn't want to wake you," said Lacey. "What's up with this doll?"

Frank gave a nervous chuckle. "Found it on the sidewalk yesterday, I was going to take it to Goodwill."

Lacey handed the doll to him as she walked past and laughed. "Uh Dad, I doubt Goodwill would want it, it's better off in the trash. Which is where Goodwill will toss it. But there was this cool pen inside. Darn thing leaked over my hand," she said, showing her hand to him where the ink had stained four thick lines, one longer than the rest, between her thumb and finger. "Now I don't have to get a tat," she said humorously.

She pranced into the house, leaving Frank standing paralyzed in the driveway, holding the doll.

###

A server brought three cups of coffee and sat them on the table. Once he left, Frank continued his story.

"It started almost immediately," Frank somberly said, pouring cream in his coffee with his shaking hand. "She was sitting on the sofa, watching something funny on television. I heard her laughing like she normally would do. Then she screamed. I thought that maybe she saw a spider or a bug. I went in, she was slumped over and she wasn't breathing. I called 9-1-1, paramedics showed up and began working on her, and out of the blue, she woke up. They checked her out and she was fine. But she wasn't."

Frank wiped the tears that flooded his eyes and continued to explain, "When Lacey woke, I held her hand and noticed that those four lines on her hand were darker than when she first showed me."

Quinn was listening attentively to Frank, sympathizing with his every word.

"She started to change," he said. "She was irritable, everything became a problem. No matter what it was, she complained about it. It wasn't like her. Lacey was always polite, to everyone. Her language became foul. She even stopped eating."

Quinn looked at Park and said, "Riley is doing the same thing. She has the same marks on her hand, between her thumb and finger, and she hasn't eaten since the kidnapping."

"I waited and waited for something to overcome me, for the 'magic' to happen, but it didn't. It was happening to Lacey, those lines on her hand posed as proof. It was the ink, from the pen, the blood of Ostar, but I didn't know its purpose yet," he softly said, bowing his head.

"She found a pen in the doll and the ink spilled on her. Pens do tend to spill ink," Park said, bored with his story.

"Not like this. The following week, when Lacey left to start her last year of college, I noticed the doll missing, she took it."

"What's the significance of the doll?" Quinn asked.

"Nothing from what I can tell other than it is what carries and protects the pen," replied Frank. "But it was then that I heard about the first suicide at her school, someone from her sorority, she jumped from the roof of the sorority house. Days later, there was another suicide. He wasn't from the university but he was connected to my daughter. A man rear-ended Lacey's car on the freeway. I got a call from our insurance company, saying something about the man having words with her and things becoming violent. They said for no reason, he suddenly hopped over the divider and walked directly into oncoming traffic."

"Sounds like a coincidence," said Park.

"Yes, that is what I thought or rather hoped. I visited Lacey at school shortly before any of the deaths occurred. She told me about problems she was having with a couple of the girls at her school, she was terribly angry, saying things she would have never said before. After the deaths, I knew that whatever was to happen to me, happened to her. My daughter was like a stranger. Ostar tricked me, he lied to me. I'm a fool, it wasn't magic, it was a curse. Instead of me giving just my soul to him, he wanted me to carry his curse that would force others to commit suicide. I now know that is what he meant when he said he wanted forfeited souls. Lacey was doing this, for him. After the third suicide, I had to stop her. My guess was that the fourth soul was to be hers. I was right."

"Wow, this is a lot to take in. You thought you were given magic by some sort of prophet when instead, you were given a curse, and you made a deal with a devil that ultimately was placed on your kid, with ink from a pen," said Park in disbelief. "Being on the other end of that story, you have to understand how much trouble I am having buying this."

"The third victim was a girl from one of Lacey's classes. I found Lacey shortly after and I chased her. When I caught her, she threw the doll, with the pen inside, over a fence. It landed in the back of a truck that was passing."

"Riley and Dylan said the doll they found fell out of an old truck," stated Quinn.

"Your child has the pen," Frank quickly responded.

Park noticed that Quinn was staring into space.

"Quinn, where are you?" asked Park. "What are you

thinking?"

"Riley has the same marks, she has the same doll, the two men that kidnapped her are supposed suicide victims, and she's behaving as Frank's daughter did," she paused for a moment. "Park, she came home with one of the bags that we used to pay the ransom. Shortly after, we heard about Troy Reynold's death and now, this man finds the doll at that cabin. This is not all coincidence! My daughter was there! She has this curse!"

"Come on! This is ridiculous!"

"It's all true and I need your help to stop it," Frank blurted. "Look at the marks on her hand. Two will already be faint because she found two souls, the two men that kidnapped her. There's one left that is the same length as the others and after that, Riley will go to Ostar, as my Lacey did. Remember, forfeited souls, human sacrifice by the blood of Ostar will revive his realm."

Park chuckled. "You're believing this?" he asked Quinn.

"Why would two low life thieves kill themselves after getting one million dollars each? That doesn't make any sense. So, yes, I believe this," Quinn replied. "Frank, what does this pen look like?"

Park was tired of the conversation, he took his wallet from his pocket and plucked out several bills. He threw them on the table and stood. "We listened and now we have to go."

Frank reached into his jacket pocket and pulled out a folded sheet of paper. He opened it revealing a sketch of the pen. He slid it to Quinn.

"This is what it looks like, it's nothing I've ever seen before. My drawing isn't the best but it's what I can remember."

Quinn took the paper and studied it.

"Your last name... Saire," Frank said to Park. "I believe your sister, Piper, attended the same university as my daughter."

Park's attention was immediately drawn to Frank.

"Oh?" he responded with a frown.

There was awkward silence as the men stared at one another. Quinn sat confused, shifting her eyes from one man to the other.

"I'm truly sorry for your loss," he said to Park as he stood.

He handed Quinn a slip of paper with his contact information and said, "Please, there isn't much time. Check your daughter's hand," he said, leaving the two in the restaurant.

"Sorry for your loss? Why would he say that to you?" Quinn questioned.

Park fell into thought. "My sister, Piper, died about three weeks ago."

"My God, I'm sorry? How?" said Quinn with compassion.

"She... She killed herself. Jumped off the roof of her sorority house."

Quinn gave a surprised expression as her mouth dropped open. "She's the first woman that he spoke of. What other reason would he say that?"

Park gave a nervous chuckle. "I think it is called coincidence and lots of surfing online. This is just a crazy man wanting attention. Come on."

Park dropped Quinn off and dashed home. His mind was running rapid with curiosity of Frank's daughter and a possible connection between her and his sister. He stepped down into the basement and to the corner where his sister's possessions were stacked in several clear plastic bins.

Piper's death was still new, and he had barely mourned her death. He was too angry at her to mourn. With a twelve-year gap in age, they had little in common, and as Piper grew into a young woman, he assumed the role of being her protector. Whatever Piper was up to, he knew about it, at least he thought.

There were no signs that Piper was suicidal. She was an open book and had a passion for whatever life threw at her. Everyone knew how happy she was, which is what made the cause of her death so devastating. She was not a candidate to take her life, is what he kept saying to himself, yet she plunged from the roof of the sorority house at her own will and with no warning, while several witnesses caught it on camera.

Had Park not seen video of her tragic death, he would have never believed that she would kill herself. Why she did it, remained a mystery.

He went through bin after bin until he came across a photo album. He lifted it and studied the cover that displayed a picture of Piper with her college friends.

Piper loved cataloging special moments of her life in customized photo books. At the end of every year since junior high, she would upload all of her pictures from the year and create a photo album. Park put the book that was created last year under his arm, glanced at the mess he made and walked up the stairs.

He poured orange juice from the refrigerator into a glass before heading into his living room with the book. He sat comfortably in a chair and began slowly flipping through the pages that had detailed captions below each picture. Piper's eyes radiated any room and they beamed of happiness.

He examined more pages before he saw it, Piper standing between two girls. He read the caption, 'Kennedy Stone, Piper Saire and Lacey Lighton. Sisterhood at its best!'

Park shifted his eyes from Lacey's name to her face, then removed the piece of paper with Frank's name and number from his wallet, to be certain that the last name was the same, and it was. He was stunned.

Park was never able to think beyond Piper's death and had no idea that she and Lacey had any kind of connection. People were dying by suicide and no one saw it as anything other than a coincidence. With the pressure young kids have to succeed, it was all chalked up as too much stress with the inability to cope.

Park did not want to accept that Lacey was somehow possessed with a curse that was meant for Frank. He didn't believe in curses and devils, it was insane. What would make not only his sister, but also two other people within weeks take their own lives, and what would make two criminals who got away with two million dollars kill themselves, he questioned.

He snagged his tablet from the coffee table and began searching for articles on the death of the last girl that Frank spoke of. He found it, her name was Chandler Sandson, a senior who had drowned herself in a bathtub, and as with his sister, no suicide note, no signs of being troubled, nothing. He then searched for details of Lacey's death, which he immediately found in a short article.

Park placed the tablet beside him on a table and stood. He began pacing, faster and faster until, in a rage, he slid his hands across the fireplace mantle shoving the neatly arranged framed pictures and candles onto the floor. He dropped to his knees and sobbed.

After seeing the connection between Piper and Lacey, and what was happening to Quinn's child, he knew that there was more to Piper's death. He deeply sighed, picked up everything he threw on the floor, swept the broken glass and then went to work looking for more information that would help him believe the impossible, that a curse had stricken his city. At that moment, he knew he needed to see Frank again.

CHAPTER THIRTEEN

Quinn was at home sitting on her bed unable to get what was happening to her daughter out of her mind. Riley was in trouble and she was convinced that something had taken over her. She believed every word Frank said and if he were right, Riley would attack one more time before she would end her own life.

Gavin walked in from another long day of work in his usual good mood.

"Hey Honey," he said, walking past her and into the bathroom. "Did Riley's blood work come back?"

"Yes, the doctor said everything was normal, not even her blood sugar level is off," she replied, not convinced that Riley was fine.

"See, the little stinker must be sneaking food."

"But..." Quinn started to say before Gavin interrupted her.

"Did you meet with that psycho guy?"

"I don't think he is psycho. I wish you would have come with me to hear what he had to say for yourself."

Gavin poked his head out of the bathroom after removing his dress shirt. "I doubt anything he had to say would have piqued my interest, but you seem to have a lot of time on your hands if you can go riding off with your new detective friend chasing crazy stories," he said with sarcasm.

"Why are you acting like none of this is odd?" Quinn said in a reserved tone.

Gavin walked out of the bathroom and to the dresser. He snatched a pair of jeans and yanked them on.

"Here's the truth Quinn! It is odd, the whole thing doesn't make sense but here it is," he said. "I don't care. I don't care how Riley managed to show up with the money, for all we know, he could have gotten the crazy guilts and threw the bag on the front lawn and then offed himself. How ever it happened, I don't care! What matters is that Riley is alive and safe and that I got at least half of my money back."

Quinn was appalled but speechless.

"Why don't you do this Quinn, since you're all buddied up with this detective, why don't you see if you can get my other million back!"

Quinn stood in front of Gavin and stared at him, not knowing what to say. She calmly left the bedroom knowing that her struggles with confrontation weren't going to end overnight.

She slowly walked to Riley's bedroom and knocked on the door before entering. Riley was laying on her bed fiddling with her doll.

"Riley," she said, slowly entering and sitting on the edge of the bed.

"Thanks for finding my doll."

"Can I see it?"

"Sure," Riley responded, handing the doll to her.

Quinn looked at Riley's hand and saw that two of the marks were faded. She couldn't stop staring, she was in a daze that filled her with sorrow.

"What's wrong?"

Quinn began squeezing the doll, hoping to discover the pen that Frank spoke of, but she found nothing.

"Nothing Honey. I'm curious, how did you get those marks on your hand?"

Riley looked at her hand for a moment. "I'm not sure. It's kinda cool."

"I'm wondering if maybe the pen that was inside this doll could have spilled over onto your hand."

"There wasn't a pen."

Quinn became angry. "Yes, there was. Did the ink from a pen leak onto your hand? Is that how you got those marks?"

Riley said nothing, she began staring into space.

"You left the house and came back in through your window with a bag filled with money, no more games. You tell me right now where you went and how you got the bag."

Riley ignored her mother who immediately pulled her up to a sitting position.

"Tell me now! I've had enough! How did you get the bag?"

Riley became outraged. She grit her teeth as she spoke, "I went out the window because I wanted to go for a walk. I couldn't go out the front door because of the dumb ass guys watching the house. I was tired of being locked up! As for the money, when I came back, the bag was in the driveway, happy?"

Riley fell back on the bed ignoring her mother. Quinn was flustered and knew that she was lying. She stood, dropped the doll on the bed beside her and walked to the door.

"Dinner is in ten minutes. Hungry or not, be down in ten," she said with a stern voice.

Ten minutes passed, Riley was at the dinner table staring at her food. It was quiet, all that could be heard was the clanking of forks against the plates.

Ashley finally spoke, "When is Dylan coming back home?"

"He's gonna stay with his buddy Aaron for a few days. We have a lot going on and Aaron's mom was gracious enough to offer to help with his recovery while she is on vacation," said Quinn. "You can go visit him any time you like."

"He'll be safe there," said Riley, picking at the food on her plate but not eating anything.

"What in the world does that mean Riley? Safe from who?" Ashley questioned.

Gavin stood without a word with his empty plate and took it into the kitchen, returning with his wallet and keys in his hand. "I need to run to a prospective site for a few hours. Got a big presentation coming up and we need to be better prepared if we are going to win this next project."

"Yes Gavin," said Riley in an evil tone. "Why do you even bother coming home? Hope we aren't putting too big of a wrench in your success."

Gavin shook his head at Riley and then at Quinn. "I give up," was all he said before he walked out.

Ashley and Riley both stood and took their dishes and headed into the kitchen.

"Riley," Quinn called. "Put your plate on the counter. I'll wrap it up for you."

Riley hunched her shoulders and continued into the kitchen with Ashley. Ashley sat her empty plate in the sink and ran water over it before putting it in the dishwasher. She watched as Riley dumped her food in the trash. Riley gave a sneaky grin.

As Ashley was about to follow Riley up the stairs, Quinn called, "Ashley, can I see you for a minute?"

Ashley walked back to Quinn.

"What's going on with you and Riley? You are getting rather hostile towards her."

"She's the one being hostile which I know you've seen. I am trying to be nice to her because I know something is wrong, but she is making it very hard, she's just awful. By the way, she threw her food in the trash."

"Let me handle it, but for now, cut her some slack."

"Of course," Ashley replied with a weak smile as she walked away.

When Ashley was out of sight, Quinn called Frank.

"Frank, this is Quinn Rucker. Can we meet?" was all she said.

That night as Riley slept, still with erratic breathing, she began to dream.

She was in the same woods where Frank met Ostar. She was alone and instead of fear, all she had was courage as she looked around in every direction seeing the trees through the fog. The moon was bright enough to notice a man slowly walking towards her. She could hear his steps over the dried and crackling fallen leaves. It was Ostar.

"I see you when I shut my eyes," Riley said.

"I am with you on your journey," said Ostar, still sounding as if he were underwater. "You will be a part of my kingdom soon. My world will live again because of you and those like you that carry the magic."

Riley continued to gaze at the demon, hanging on to and worshiping every word he said. Ostar smiled, showing his brown stained teeth.

"One more Riley, one more that fiercely angers you. Pass the magic and then send your soul to me. Now go, your time is nearing. Finish the journey. Finish it."

Riley snapped out of her sleep and sat up. Her room was dark and quiet. She laid down and fell back asleep.

###

Quinn was desperate and filled with enough anguish to make her ache all over. She followed Frank's directions on where to meet him and the longer she drove, the more unsure she was about everything. Would anyone else believe there was a curse that had taken over Riley? Maybe Frank wasn't who she thought he was, after all, he came into their lives right after Riley found the doll and was kidnapped. What if she's falling into a trap, could she trust him? Even with doubt, she knew she had to take a chance.

She found herself outside of the city in a remote area. She parked alongside the deserted road that was surrounded by woods. Finally, she saw from her rear view mirror, headlights from a car approach, it was Frank. He parked behind her and stepped out. Quinn was reluctant to get out of her car. She rolled her window down and looked at him with dismay.

"Do you believe me?" Frank asked in desperation.

"Two of the bars on Riley's hand are faint, there's two left and I'm scared. Please, tell me what to do," she said before glancing around. "Why did you ask me to meet you here?"

"This is where I met Ostar. I wanted you to see. I was about to end it all and he showed up, standing right in front of me. I would come back regularly with hopes that he would appear and take the curse from Lacey and put it on me, obviously that wasn't how it worked, he never showed again. A soul is a soul and he didn't give a damn who delivered them to him."

"How can we stop this?" Quinn asked, getting out of her car.

"The ink from the pen, Ostar's blood. We need to destroy it. I'm thinking that it has to be human blood, pure blood as Ostar called it, that can stop this. Something I remember Ostar saying to me that night when I asked him what would happen if I changed my mind, he said something about how I couldn't because my blood wasn't pure."

"What about my blood?" Quinn questioned.

"Yes, yours. Mine isn't pure because of my sin of wanting to kill myself. At least that is what I believe."

"Finding that pen is easier said than done."

"Have you spoken to Park since we met?" he asked.

"No, but there's a connection isn't there? Between your daughter and his sister."

"Her soul went to Ostar, through Lacey. When Park learns that my daughter was the cause of his sister's death, he will believe. He wasn't going to listen to me, I gave him the hint he needed to make him realize that what I say is true."

"How did Lacey decide on the souls for Ostar?"

Quinn asked.

"Emotions of extreme revenge and anger against anyone that caused it. It is what happened to Lacey. Riley sought the souls of the kidnappers, rightly so, they angered her, and she wanted revenge. As soon as those strong emotions inside her arise, she will do it again," he said. "This is where it began. In case something happens to me, remember this place. It's the one lead we have to Ostar."

"Your wife, where is she?"

Frank bowed his head in sorrow. "Her name is Maria. She stuck with me through my gambling addiction. Even after we were about to lose it all, she stood by me. But this thing, with Lacey, the curse, the deaths, she wouldn't believe what I said. When I showed her the money that was placed in our account by Ostar, she said that I somehow finally won with a bet and wanted nothing to do with the claim I had. I couldn't touch that money, ever. I had to try to fix this, so, I left."

"I'm sorry that you have been going through this alone. You have me now."

Frank gave a grim smile and said, "Keep Riley in your sight. Keep her occupied and find that pen."

"She didn't put it back in the doll. In fact, she denies even having it."

"I'd like to meet Riley."

Quinn contemplated for a moment.

"I'm taking her to the mall tomorrow, I can text you when we are there and where to meet us."

Quinn gave a faint-hearted gaze to Frank before getting in her car. Frank got back into his car and drove away, leaving Quinn who was staring at the clear dark skies, in awe of what was happening. What she thought to always be fiction had become reality and the evil who called himself Ostar was real. She needed a miracle.

It was quiet in the house when she arrived home. All the lights were out, Gavin was still at work and figured that both Ashley and Riley were asleep. She crept up the stairs to Riley's room where she quietly cracked the door open. Riley was laying under the cover, but Quinn could see it moving from the quivering of her body. She could hear her bizarre and rapid breathing.

"Riley," she whispered, getting no response.

She gently moved the cover from Riley's face that revealed a shocking scene. Though she appeared to be asleep, her eyes were wide open. Her pupils were shimmering and her eyeballs were nearly covered in blood. Quinn gasped in terror, waking Riley whose eyes immediately went back to normal.

"Are... are you cold? " she asked in a frightened tone. "I can bring you more covers."

Riley calmly closed her eyes. Quinn stepped out of the bedroom with her hands firmly over her mouth. She ran to her room, fastened the door and fell to her bed, sobbing as softly as she could.

"This feels great getting out of the house," said Riley in a cheerful mood, prancing beside her mother in the mall.

They stopped at a clothing store and examined merchandise through the window.

"I think this is what you needed," said Quinn, trying to show excitement while remembering the horror she saw in Riley's eyes the night before. "Let's go in this store and get you a couple cool tops."

They walked into the store where Riley immediately saw shirts on a rack and bolted to it, leaving Quinn at the entrance.

"I'll be out here."

Quinn walked to the bench that was outside the store and sat. Moments later, she spotted Frank coming towards her. She stood and approached him.

"Thanks for agreeing to meet me," Frank said. "I need to see her."

"She's in there."

"Let's go."

"We should wait until she is finished. I'll bring her out to you," said Quinn, walking into the store.

"Mom!" Riley called from inside the store, holding up a t-shirt. "Can I get it?"

Quinn walked to her and examined the shirt. "Yep, you can get it."

Quinn stepped to the checkout register with the shirt and placed it on the counter where a young teen-aged girl stood talking on her cell phone. She chuckled a few times into the phone before noticing that Quinn was standing on the other side of the counter. Quinn became impatient and bothered by the teen's rudeness.

"Excuse me," she said.

The girl raised her first finger to Quinn and continued her conversation, at times giggling.

"Where's your manager?" Quinn asked in a stern tone and loud enough for the teen to end her call.

"What's your problem? I happen to be the assistant manager and geeze, I wasn't on the phone that long," she said, grabbing the shirt.

"Sorry to inconvenience you," said Quinn, annoyed at the girl. "Riley, I saw another store with this same shirt, why don't we go there."

"I don't like the lady here anyway," Riley snarled.
"How dare you treat my mother like that."

Riley yanked the shirt from the girl and threw it in her
face, causing Quinn to clench Riley's arm.

"Riley! Let's go!" she scolded, dragging her out of the
store and into the mall corridor.

"But, Mom! She was mean to you! I hate her!" she
yelled as Frank joined them. "Who are you?"

"You must be Riley," Frank cheerfully said.

"Sorry, we had a moment in the store," said Quinn,
feeling fatigued.

"Those things happen," said Frank smiling at Riley.

Riley was confused by the man. She frowned and said,
"Sure."

Frank extended his hand to Riley and said, "My name
is Frank, I am a friend of your mom's."

Riley gave a firm shake, giving Frank a chance to
quickly glance to see the familiar marks on her hand. She
snatched her hand away.

"Why that's a pretty cool tat you got. Where'd you get
it? Do you know what it means?" he asked.

"It means two down and two to go," she said
sarcastically. "I don't know."

Frank glanced at Quinn who was speechless.

"Riley, go take a seat on that bench, I need to talk to
Frank for a minute."

Frank and Quinn stepped a couple yards away.

"She definitely is carrying this curse. I'm scared. How
do I convince anyone of this? No one will believe it.
Gavin won't even listen to any of what I say."

"This is up to us."

Suddenly, there was a screech from inside the store
that Quinn and Riley were in. Quinn saw that Riley was

no longer sitting on the bench. She and Frank ran into the store where Riley had leaped on the counter and lunged at the teenager who was desperately punching and kicking, even throwing merchandise at the crazed girl making it impossible for Riley to grasp her face. Frank sprinted to the counter to try to free the girl from Riley's incredible strength.

"Riley! Stop!" Quinn yelled, shoving the child several times until she released the girl.

Riley was breathing like a wild animal. Quinn wrapped her arms around her and held her tightly.

"Relax, slow breaths."

Riley put her arms around her mother who was in tears while Frank consoled the mortified girl.

"I hate her," Riley whispered in Quinn's ear. "I hate her so much."

CHAPTER FOURTEEN

Park was at his desk in the police station searching for information from his computer. A fellow detective and friend approached. His name was Milo Savatt, he was an average looking dark skinned black man who was slightly older than Park.

"What's going on? Working on your day off?" Milo asked scratching his bald head.

"Hey Milo, you do know that there's never a day off in the world of crime," he said with humor while reading a document. "I was reading the report on Piper. I know it was ruled a suicide but..."

Milo was blunt and said, "It's a fact Park. And this is no way to heal from her death."

"There was another girl, her name was Chandler Sandson, she went to the same university and died about a week ago. She took her own life too. I think there may be a connection between both of their deaths, and I think that connection was Lacey Lighton."

"Who also committed suicide," Milo added. "Yes, I know, I responded to that call. What are you getting at?"

"I wanted to learn more about them to see if, or how, they connected. I was so caught up with Piper that it never dawned on me that they were from the same sorority, maybe because Lacey wasn't on campus when she died."

"What good is this doing? You need to keep Piper's memory alive and move on, not dig into stuff you may never find answers to."

"Look," Park said, pointing to an Instagram post showing several pictures of Piper and girls from her school, including Lacey.

"It's just a bunch of kids doing stupid kid stuff," he said.

"What about this? These posts were from Piper the day before she died. Listen to this. 'Don't always believe what Lacey says, she has a way to show how fake she can be. Watch your back ladies.' And then here's a comment that Lacey posted. 'Wow Pipe! Let's get our facts straight before we start calling people out. If it walks like a slut... Need I say more?"

"Hm," said Milo, puzzled. "Young kid junk, I wish they'd never come up with all this social media crap. What are you getting at?"

Park opened another page. "This one is from Chandler's page, she wasn't in the sorority but they had the same group of friends," he said as he opened photos from her social media page showing that Lacey was in several.

"I'll be damned," said Milo. "Can you see any of her posts?"

"Yep, already did and this is interesting, here," Park responded, opening a comment. "Chandler seems to be passive-aggressive but Lacey picked up on it. This is what Lacey said, 'It doesn't surprise me that Chandler would be saying crap about me, such a hater. If I were her, I'd be jealous too.' She died the day after that post."

"Wow," Milo said. "There was a lot of tension between Lacey and your sister, and Chandler. But Lacey also killed herself, who connects her to that?"

"That's the number one question, but you gotta see that there's something strange going on, and did you know that Lacey was involved in a car accident that happened between Chandler's and Piper's deaths?"

Milo raised a brow.

"I read the report. The other party involved was a man who witnesses say got pissed off at her. He pushed her around a bit, blaming her for the accident. Lacey fought back, she clawed him in the face, and then all of a sudden, the man stopped fighting and walked into oncoming traffic, on the freeway. He was hit several times before cars finally stopped. But the point is, Lacey was connected to that suicide too, then oddly enough she kills herself not even an hour after Chandler's death."

Milo was without question, interested in what Park was telling him. "But still, what we don't have is who is connected to Lacey's suicide. We should check this out."

"It's probably nothing, I had to see if any dots connected. I guess I'm trying to find closure."

"We could always discuss it with the captain," Milo said with a grin appearing. "Maybe you and I can partner up on this, like old times."

"Nah, it's fine," Park said in a dismissive manner.

Park and Milo had been good friends for several

years. Park told him everything that was happening in his life, which is why it was so easy for him to ramble on about connections with the deaths. Before he knew it, he had said more than he wanted and realized that he could not involve Milo.

"You're right, digging through this isn't helping. This is all a coincidence, I know that," said Park.

"Okay," Milo said, scratching his head somewhat confused. "Hey, how did it go with your visit with Mr. Rucker? You know, I can work this case with you if you want. You don't have to do everything solo."

Park thought for a moment. "No lead from seeing Mr. Rucker. Cobson was a janitor and way too low on the pole for someone as arrogant as Mr. Rucker to know he even existed," he said, typing on his computer keyboard. He wasn't a good liar and if Milo saw his face, he'd know.

"Sounds like you're still at square one on where that money came from."

"It is still a mystery," answered Park.

"I'm here if you need another set of eyes. Oh, I almost forgot, I doubt you want to hear this, but I ran into Samantha at the post office. She asked how you were and to tell you hi."

Park became unsettled. "You could have told her you would pass that along without actually telling me."

"Come on, you could at least be civil to her," said Milo.

"She left me at the altar. After four years together, you'd think she would have walked away a long time ago and saved me the embarrassment."

"She's sorry. She said she's been trying to reach you since it all happened. Eight months is a long time to keep holding this grudge. She heard about Piper, left you messages and nothing," Milo informed.

"Why are you all of a sudden on her side? The damage is done," Park said, still peering at his computer screen.

"And why can't you forgive. At least you didn't marry her and then get a divorce. It sucks that it went down that way but..."

"But what? I was all in Milo and when I'm all in, that's exactly what I am. She went into our relationship knowing exactly who I was, and to think I would give up my career because she expected me to, is crazy. She shouldn't have assumed that I would change. She knew that wasn't going to happen and I never led her to believe any different. She was just too insecure. She wanted me to quit my career. Would have been great if she realized that it was a deal breaker before our wedding day."

"I get it Park. Sorry I mentioned it," Milo said, walking away.

Park exited the sites and began reading Lacey's autopsy report. His eyes froze on a description of her right hand and the description of the faded bars that were between her thumb and finger. He began to think about what Frank said and how Quinn expressed the same on Riley's hand. How true could the story be that Frank told?

Gavin was busy working in his den when he heard a knock on the door.

"Come in," he said as the door opened. It was Jack.

"Ashley let me in," Jack said, taking a seat in front of Gavin's desk. "I am sorry that I wasn't able to call you back. We were in the middle of nowhere on a surveillance. No service. Figured I'd head over on my way home."

"It's about time you showed up. I called you several times," Gavin said with a grin. "I don't even want to know how you managed this but thank you. You'll have a sweet bonus in your check. I'll call it a project completion bonus."

Jack was confused. He got comfortable in his seat and crossed his legs. "I'll bite," he said. "Managed what?"

Gavin chuckled. "I'm not thrilled that we got only half of the money back and curious as to why you didn't grab the first bag of money out of that guy's trunk. I'm thinking maybe you were going for it, but someone showed up. I don't know, but half is much better than nothing. I don't think I'll be able to retrieve it, but just the same, you got rid of the goons and they won't be bothering us again."

Jack scratched his head, then leaned forward. "Gavin, what the hell are you talking about?"

Gavin's grin faded. "The money, my money."

"My men were able to locate one of the guys after he purchased that vehicle, but when my men were able to find him, it was too late to do anything."

"What? And what about the other guy?"

"I have no clue, we got a hit only on the guy that bought the Porsche."

Gavin stood.

"Jack! Don't play games with me. Riley crawled in her bedroom window with the bag from the other guy and he's dead. Suicide," he said with a raised voice. "You're telling me that you didn't have anything to do with that either? You didn't give it to her? You didn't make both of these men's deaths look like suicide?"

"That's exactly what I'm telling you. I don't know anything about the other guy or how Riley wound up with any money," Jack said, standing. "I love the idea of getting a big bonus, but I have done nothing. Sorry."

"This is odd."

"I don't know what to say."

"I thought you did it," said Gavin.

"That's a bit of a sloppy job for me to take credit. Just be happy that you have half of your money back. I'll pull my men off surveillance from the house and the kid's school. You obviously cannot go to the police and tell them the money is yours," said Jack as he walked to the door and opened it. "On Monday, we update your home security. State of the art."

"I am heading to Houston tonight, but Quinn will be here and very happy about the security."

Quinn arrived at the door of Gavin's den as Jack was leaving.

"Hey Quinn," Jack greeted. "Have a good day."

"Hello Jack," said Quinn as Jack walked away.

Quinn stepped in and noticed a baffled expression on Gavin's face.

"What's going on? What's wrong?"

"Sit down," he instructed.

"You're scaring me," Quinn said as she slowly sat in the chair in front of Gavin's desk.

Gavin walked around his desk and sat in another chair beside her.

"The ransom money, it was marked. I told Jack to do whatever to get my money back and to take care of those guys. I thought he was behind both of their deaths, but he wasn't."

"Riley did it," she blurted.

"I'm not going that far to believe our twelve-year-old daughter killed the men that kidnapped her. It was suicide!"

"You have to listen to what Frank has to say."

Gavin sighed. "It may always be a mystery about the money. We need to put it past us."

"We can't put it past us. What's happening to Riley happened to Frank's daughter. It's a curse Gavin! Riley killed those men and she's going to do it again!"

Gavin laughed. "You're kidding. Either that or you're crazy. A curse?"

"Do not talk to me like that! Do not belittle me! Ever again!" Quinn shouted. "Frank's daughter is responsible for Park's sister's death and after she killed her, she killed herself! Riley will kill again, she will do it one more time before she takes her own life. Yes! It sounds crazy but it's the truth and I need your help. You can't leave for Houston, you can't!"

"I'll be back the day after tomorrow Quinn. You gotta get this junk out of your head. There's no curse. Please, get your head straight. The kids need you while I am gone."

Quinn jumped from the chair in anger throwing her hands up. She swung the door open and slammed it behind her, leaving Gavin sitting in awe.

Quinn spent most of the day watching movies with Riley. She didn't want to leave her but seeing the bars on Riley's hand brought her back to her horrid reality and she knew she had to leave her one more time. She checked her watch.

"I'll be back," Quinn said as she stood from the couch.

She walked to the kitchen and dialed a number on her cell phone.

"Frank, are you at the hotel? Okay, I'll be there in an hour," she said before disconnecting the call.

"Ashley," Quinn called.

"I'm upstairs," Ashley responded.

Quinn jogged up the stairs to Ashley who was folding bed sheets in the linen pantry.

"Ashley," she whispered. "I don't have time to explain but I need you to not get Riley angry."

Ashley frowned. "What?"

"Please, do as I say. Just keep her in a good mood. Okay?"

"Sure," Ashley replied thinking how odd Quinn's request was.

"I gotta run out for a bit. Riley is watching a movie but I'll be back shortly, thank you," Quinn said, trotting back down the stairs.

"After her movie we'll go hang out in the hot tub," said Ashley from the top of the stairs.

Quinn swung her purse over her shoulder and went back to Riley.

"Riley, there's a small problem with the plans we made for the society dinner. I need to run out and get it taken care of, but I will be back soon. After the movie, grab your suit. Ashley would love to go in the hot tub with you."

"Okay," Riley replied, continuing to watch and laugh at the movie.

"I love you so much," she said, gently kissing her forehead.

###

On that dreadful day when the call went out over the police radio of his sister's death, Park drove like a mad man recklessly through the downtown streets to the sorority house where she lived. He saw her lying face down on the pavement in a pool of blood. It was the kind of shock he always saw others in after seeing a loved one dead, but he never expected to have to experience it himself.

He remembered running to her, dropping to the ground and holding her in his arms. When it was time to move her body, it took three officers to pry his grip from her.

He watched Piper's body as it was laid on a gurney and rolled into the coroner's van. Not a tear was shed from his eyes, in fact, he never cried, not even at her funeral. He was numb.

A week after Piper died, Park went back to work. His heart was empty and he found it hard to concentrate, but staying home and doing nothing, was worse. Park couldn't focus on the cases he was assigned causing his captain to place him back on leave. He needed time to grieve, but something was keeping him from doing so.

Park spent another week off work trying to get his head straight and to rid the guilt he had for not seeing that Piper had a problem. He thought he knew everything about her. She told him everything, sharing things that he didn't want to know. But that showed him how much she trusted him and how close they were. For days, he thought there was another side of Piper who lived with emotional pain, when in fact she was not in pain at all.

He buried Piper next to their parent's empty lots, expecting them to be first. Piper was in her last year of college and ready to face the world, but instead, he stood in front of her grave where tears finally fell from his eyes.

"Pipe, I thought that there was something hurting you so bad that you couldn't tell me. I was angry for what you did," he softly said.

He wiped tears from his face and took a deep breath.
"You jumped, but you didn't want to do it. I know
that now. I know you didn't take your life the way they
said you did. It was Lacey, but it wasn't her fault either. A
thing, a devil, took you away from us... They call him
Ostar. I know it sounds too crazy to believe, but it's true.
I don't know how, but he's going to pay for what he's
done... what he's doing. You see, there's a family out there
in trouble because of this. I know you'd want me to do
whatever I could to help them. I wish it wasn't, but this is
real."

It was night when Frank opened his hotel suite door,
surprised but happy to see Park standing, humble, in
front of him.

"Come in Park, you don't know how happy I am to
see you," Frank greeted, gesturing for him to enter.
"Quinn is here."

Quinn was standing with a small glass half-filled with
whiskey.

"Change of heart? Whatever the case, I'm glad you are
here too," said Quinn, pouring another drink and handing
it to him.

"Thanks, I have the feeling we're going to need many
of these. Whatever this is, devil, demon, it took my sister,
and Frank's child, and it's about to take Riley. Whatever it
is, I need to help stop it."

Frank stood in front of Park and placed his hand on
his shoulder in remorse. "I am sorry, this is my fault."

"If it wasn't you, it would have been someone else. It
was someone else a hundred years ago. We need to focus

on what's about to happen next if we can't stop this."

"I think I know how," said Frank, relieved that Park didn't do anything drastic like punch him in his face. "I think that if we can find the pen, somehow get it open and add a drop of your blood or Quinn's blood to it, it may end the curse. But I can't say for sure."

"Who's to say that if we succeed at this, that he won't bring another curse?" questioned Park. "I can't believe that I'm even asking this."

"I don't know," replied Frank. "If I remember correctly, this may be his one chance to bring back his realm. I hope I am right."

"Let's work on what we do know. Riley's got one bar left before she takes her life," said Quinn. "She must have the pen on her and I don't know how I can get it."

"We have to try and it won't be easy," Frank replied. "You need to keep Riley away from as many people as possible. The less she is around people the less chance someone can anger her, we saw what she did at the mall."

"When do we do this?" asked Quinn in determination. "I can't lose her."

"There's one soul left before she gives hers," said Frank. "I say now. Quinn, she still comes to you and she won't take your soul."

"Why is that?" Park asked, downing the rest of his drink.

"She cannot possess those that have her blood. That's why she didn't take Quinn's son. She tried and she hurt him, but she couldn't make him kill himself."

"I can't be gone for too much longer, I left my niece, Ashley with Riley, I told her not to do anything that would make her angry," Quinn said, becoming anxious. "But I should still head back."

"Remember Quinn, she can't take her soul, Ashley is

her aunt."

"Gavin is Riley's stepfather, there's no blood relation between she and Ashley," she explained, grabbing her bag.

"Go get her out. If Ashley were to infuriate her..." Frank took a deep breath and exhaled. "We'll be close behind. Park do you have a Taser or something we can use to slow her down?"

"Yes, we'll need to make a quick stop at my house," Park answered.

"Quinn, what about your husband?"

"Gavin is leaving on a business trip tonight," Quinn said, checking her watch. "He has already left for the airport."

"Once we have the pen, we won't be able to keep her down for long, if at all, we'll have to move fast."

"Yeah and pray the pen actually opens," Park said, trying to show humor as they rushed out of the hotel room.

CHAPTER FIFTEEN

Ashley was relaxing in the hot tub while Riley stood along the side watching her. Music was playing from a portable speaker where the sound cut in and out.

"Riley, the water is great, why won't you join me? Remember when we would sit out here forever gazing at the stars and you would tell me all the kid gossip at your school?"

Riley continued to watch her.

"Riley, I know that what you have been through is horrible and I'm sorry," she said, moving the water back and forth with her hands. "I know your parents are having a hard time too trying to figure out how to handle all of this."

"They aren't having a hard time and I only have one parent. Gavin happens to be married to my mom and he cares about his company and his money more than anything else. I got some of it back to shut him up. My mom loves him, that's why I try to keep him off limits, cause she's weak and needs him. It's my choice."

"What? What does that even mean?"

Riley said nothing. Ashley chuckled with humor.

Riley rolled her eyes. "My mom is too weak to figure out how to handle anything. I feel sorry for her."

Riley's comments surprised Ashley. "That isn't a fair statement about your mother. You know all she wants is happiness for you and your brother, she would do anything for you," said Ashley in a defensive tone. "What's going on with you? This rude behavior of yours started after..."

"After those assholes took me, yes I know."

"Do you want to talk about it?"

"To who?"

"I'm here," Ashley said with sincerity, "I'm always here Riley."

Riley stepped to the deck of the hot tub and sat. She flicked the water with her fingers. "You are?" she asked.

"Of course, can we talk about Dylan? What's going on between you two?"

The music from the speaker stopped and Ashley became annoyed.

"Darn it, battery died. I forgot to plug it in," she said, before speaking again to Riley. "Why did you hurt him?"

A nerve was struck inside Riley's head. She became angry and abruptly turned her head away from Ashley.

"I didn't hurt him!" she shouted in anger as her eyes filled with blood and her pupils flashed explosive sparks.

Once her eyes became normal, she faced Ashley again.

"You were smiling like you were glad."

"No, I wasn't smiling," Riley responded, trying to

keep control.

"You need to come clean to your parents about it and apologize to your brother."

"I'm not sorry for anything, you bitch! You didn't see me do anything! Who cares that I smiled! Why can't you leave it alone!"

"You are so disrespectful! I know it's been hard, but don't take it out on us!"

"You're right," Riley said in a sneaky tone.

"There's my Riley. Can you do me a favor? I brought an extension cord out to charge my speaker, it's already in the wall, would you please plug my speaker cord in?"

Riley gave a devious grin before prancing to the speaker and plugging the cord into the extension. She then skipped back to Ashley and leaned in to her with her arms open.

"I'm sorry Ashley, can I have a hug?"

Ashley opened her dripping arms and embraced Riley for a brief second before Riley clutched her face and slit her cheek with her thumbnail. She moved back and watched as Ashley stepped out of the hot tub, in a trance.

It was at that moment, Quinn arrived home. She ran from her car to the front door, swinging it open and stopping in the foyer with an uneasy feeling.

"Hey! Are you two outside?" Quinn called, hearing nothing but the faint sound of music coming from the backyard. She trotted to the back of the house and out the patio door.

"I thought I'd never get..." she started to say before seeing Ashley moving, as if she were sleep walking, to the patio table where she lifted her speaker attached to the extension cord and headed back to the hot tub.

Still in a slumber, Ashley treaded into the hot tub while Riley watched with a sneer.

"Ashley no!" Quinn shrieked as she sprinted to the outlet, unplugging it from the wall before Ashley dropped it into the water.

Quinn ran to Ashley and began violently shaking her, but she would not snap out of her stupor.

"Riley! What have you done!"

Riley's eyes shimmered brightly, then faded before she ran into the house. Quinn helped Ashley away from the hot tub and onto the grass. She sat her down and continued to shake her until she began gasping for air.

"Ashley! Ashley! Can you hear me?"

Quinn was distraught, though she stopped Ashley from killing herself, she knew she would try again.

"My blood," Quinn whispered, breathing heavy. She frantically slung her purse that was strapped over her shoulder to the ground.

"Hang on Ash," she said, fumbling for her keys.

Once she found her key chain, she quickly pierced her palm with one of the keys, grunting from the pain. She closed her hand to allow the blood to fill in her palm and held it to Ashley's face. She watched her blood trickle into Ashley's wound. In an instant, Ashley snapped from her daze, confused.

"Can you understand me?" Quinn asked, pushing the hair from Ashley's face.

Ashley coughed. "Yes, what happened?"

She touched her face and wiped her hand across her wound. She saw the blood on her hand and began to panic.

"What happened! How did I get this cut?" she cried.

Quinn snatched a robe that sat on a lawn chair and draped it over her.

"Listen, you cannot go back in the house. Here," she

said, holding her keys to Ashley. "I can't explain now but you have to get out of here. Go around the side to my car, get in and drive yourself to Aaron's, where Dylan is staying. His mother can fix your wound, just don't tell her what happened."

She took the keys, still dazed.

"Ashley, listen to me! Riley did this to you. Can you stand?" she asked, pulling her up.

Ashley nodded.

"You have to go!"

Ashley was disoriented. "Okay," she muttered.

"Go! You're going to be fine," Quinn said, grabbing Ashley's phone from the patio table and giving it to her. "I will call you as soon as I can."

Ashley stumbled across the grass in her bare feet to the side of the house and out of the gate to Quinn's car. She got in and screeched away.

Quinn was terrified. She crept into the house from the back patio where she called Park.

"Park," she frantically whispered. "You two need to get here now! Ashley is safe. Riley is in the house. I'll keep her concentrating on me so that you can get to her room, in case the pen isn't on her. Come through the front. Please hurry."

Quinn shoved her phone back in her pocket and took a deep breath.

"Riley," she called. "Honey, I'm not mad, I want to help you. You know how much I love you."

Riley stepped to the top of the staircase.

"You shouldn't have stopped her Quinn."

"Honey, come to me. Let's figure this out," Quinn said as she extended her hand up to her. "I know how to help you. Let me help."

Riley took a couple steps down before she stopped.

"What's wrong?" Quinn asked. "Come to me."

"You are mad. I know that you are."

"No, of course I'm not, this isn't your fault Riley. None of it. I can't lose you, you need to fight this. If you give me the pen, I can help you. You can have your life back. Don't you want your life back?"

Riley's eyes flashed.

"You can't stop it!" she screamed. "Go away! Ostar cannot be stopped. He doesn't want to take our world, he's trying to save his, and we can help him."

"This is wrong. Please, come down and let me hold you."

Riley began to walk down the stairs and stopped a couple steps from the floor in front of Quinn, whose eyes were flooded with tears.

"My soul is for Ostar," she said as the whites of her eyes filled with blood. This time it didn't disappear.

Quinn reached for her and held her tightly. She began rubbing her as she would always do, but this time, patting her body, searching for the pen. Riley pushed away from her.

"It's not on me," she said.

"Wha... What are you talking about?"

She shoved Quinn to the floor. "I don't want to hurt you but you're leaving me no choice Quinn!"

Suddenly, Gavin unexpectedly walked in the front door, curious as to why it was open.

"Honey! Why is the door open? I changed my flight. I felt bad about our last conversation. I'm willing to listen..."

He halted when he saw, beyond the foyer, Quinn standing at the staircase with Riley. Riley immediately stepped back up the stairs when she saw him.

"What's going on?"

"Gavin, she's dangerous!" Quinn cried.

"What the hell!" Gavin exclaimed, horrified at the sight of Riley's blood red eyes.

Riley brushed past Quinn and tackled Gavin and in no time, she scratched his face with her fingernail and pushed him away. She stood in front of him, watching with eagerness as his face went blank. Blood trickled from the wound on his cheek. He stood and headed for the kitchen. Quinn ran behind him grabbing at him, but he was too strong for her to hold.

"Gavin stop! She wants you to do this. Don't!"

Gavin reached the kitchen counter and slid out a large straight edge blade from the knife rack. Quinn saw that there was not enough blood coming from the cut in her palm to save him, and before she could do anything, he put the knife to his throat and ran it across his neck. He dropped it and immediately fell to the floor.

Quinn was petrified, there was nothing she could do for Gavin and she knew she had to stay focused, for Riley's sake. Her life was about to end if she couldn't find a way to stop her.

When Park and Frank arrived at the house, they peered through the window at the front door to see the back of Riley who was still facing the kitchen. She observed Quinn who was kneeling beside Gavin and sobbing. Both men quietly pushed the already partially opened door and tiptoed in and up the stairs, peeking in every room until they found Riley's.

"We have to hurry," Frank whispered, entering Riley's room. "The bed, she left the doll."

Park picked up the doll from her bed and gave it to Frank who began feeling around for the pen. It wasn't there.

"Damn it!" Frank softly exclaimed.

Park noticed Riley's doll case and carefully examined each doll until he saw one slightly out of line with the others.

"There," Park said, clutching the back of a chair and dragging it in front of the case. "That one is not in place like the rest. It's gotta be in that one."

Park jumped on the chair, opened the case and removed the doll. Its head was made of porcelain and the body was made of thick felt. He tossed it to Frank who ripped open the back and saw what he'd been searching for. The pen was buried deep in the material of the doll.

"When I got the doll from Lacey and touched the pen, she went mad. Riley will undoubtedly do the same," Frank said.

"Do it," Park ordered.

As soon as Frank touched the pen, an alarm of shock ran through Riley's body and she immediately realized that it was in someone else's possession. She roared and ran up the stairs like a savage, skipping several steps. Quinn ran after her and by the time she was half way up the stairs, Riley already made it up to her bedroom where she faced the men with balled fists.

"Riley, I know you need this," Frank said, holding the pen up. "Ostar can't have my soul. The last bar is for you."

Quinn rushed into the bedroom and stood behind Riley. "Riley please! We are here to help you!"

"Give it to me!" she screamed. "I can still kill you!"

Frank shoved the pen into the original doll and threw it to Quinn. "Go!" he yelled as Riley lunged at him.

Park tried to help pull the girl from Frank as Quinn ran out of the room. Enraged, Riley shoved both men from her and ran out, sniffing for Quinn's scent. She checked both directions and barreled to the master bedroom.

Park and Frank dashed after Riley who had burst into Quinn's bedroom. Quinn nervously stuffed the doll in the back of her pants.

"Riley, listen to me. It's Mom."

Riley stood before Quinn in a rage. "Give it back! I have to finish the journey! Ostar needs me to do my part!"

"Riley, fight! Fight this! Don't let Ostar win! You can do this," Quinn pleaded out of breath.

Riley let out a shriek and rushed to Quinn who quickly yanked the doll from her pants and threw it over Riley where it landed on the floor at Frank's feet. He picked it up as if it was a sick game of Keep Away and fled out of the room. Park and Quinn wrestled with Riley hoping they could hold her off long enough for Frank to snag the pen from the doll and figure out how to open it, but Riley was so strong that no amount of people could hold her down.

"Stop Riley!" Quinn yelled, grabbing Riley's arm.

Riley bit Quinn's forearm. She cried in pain, releasing the child allowing her to head-butt Park and push him aside.

Frank ran down the stairs carrying the doll under his arm, pulling and tugging at the pen that would not open.

"Park! Quinn!" Frank called from the bottom of the stairs. "Stop! Let me talk to her! Riley! Riley!"

Quinn and Park watched as Riley walked to the top of the staircase and looked down at Frank.

"You have almost fulfilled your obligation to Ostar," said Frank, holding the doll up to allow her to see him place the pen back inside. "You need this. You need to pass the curse before you send your soul to him. I have it."

Park and Quinn stood quietly watching as Riley slowly took one step down the stairs before throwing herself on Frank, causing him to drop the doll. She wrapped her legs around Frank's neck. He struggled desperately to break free, but she was too strong.

Park snatched the Taser from the back of his pants, aimed and shot Riley in her back. It was only seconds of convulsing before Riley yanked the darts from her skin. She was still holding Frank with her legs and snapped his neck as easy as breaking a pencil in two. She jumped to her feet with the doll firmly in her hand.

"Riley no!" Quinn hysterically shouted, running down the stairs behind Park in pursuit of the elusive girl.

Riley rushed past Frank and over Gavin's body, charging forward through the glass patio door, shattering it. Park and Quinn sprang out of the glassless frame behind her to the end of the property where the creek ran. Riley fiercely hurled the doll, with the pen inside, down and into the creek several yards away where the mildly rapid waters immediately sucked it in and washed it away.

"No!" Quinn yelled.

Park sprinted past Riley and into the water where he splashed around desperately searching for the doll. Riley hurried past Quinn and back into the house.

Quinn ran after her and up the stairs to the master bedroom. As Quinn entered, she saw Riley standing outside on the ledge of the deck.

"Riley, please, please don't do this," Quinn begged as she slowly approached the child.

"Riley's gone," she said as her pupils no longer

sparkled and the blood disappeared from her eyes. "She's about to be a part of Ostar."

"No no no! Riley fight!"

"Is what it is," was all Riley said before she let herself fall from the balcony.

Quinn jumped to catch her and fell over the ledge behind Riley. Riley landed on the cement beside the pool and Quinn fell on top of Riley's already dead body.

Park waded down the creek hoping that he would find the doll, but it was gone. He made his way to an embankment, out of the water and back to the house where he saw Quinn on top of Riley.

He knelt and saw that Quinn was still breathing. He gently moved her from Riley then pulled his cell phone from his pocket.

"Don't move Quinn, I'm calling for help," he said with the phone to his ear.

Quinn's ear was bleeding and she spit up blood. "Riley," she softly sniveled. "Riley."

Quinn passed out, giving Park the chance to glance at the girl that laid beside her mom, lifeless.

Ostar had again succeeded, this time through Riley. His realm received three more souls along with Riley's, whose forfeited soul went to Ostar making him stronger and bringing his realm another step closer to life.

Quinn fell unconscious, which was good, Park thought. He didn't want to tell her that Riley was dead and the doll that carried the blood of Ostar washed away.

Quinn woke hours later in a hospital bed, Park was asleep in a chair in a corner. She blinked over and over until her blurred vision was gone.

"Park," she moaned. "Park."

Park awakened and quickly moved to her side. "Hey, how do you feel? You were lucky considering. Concussion, some broken ribs, punctured lung and a broken arm. A lot of bruises, but you're going to be fine."

"What happened? Riley went out the window and..." she said, becoming agitated. "She went off the ledge!"

"I'm sorry Quinn," he said, then pausing. "She didn't make it."

Quinn felt paralyzed as tears ran down her cheeks. She began to sob. "My baby, Gavin, they're gone. How am I going to live without them?"

"I'm going to stop this," Park sternly said.

"What?"

"The doll, it went down the creek. I couldn't find it, but I will, and I'm going to find a way to stop the curse. Your daughter, my sister, Gavin and Frank. Gone for what reason? No one will believe this story. Hell, I didn't believe it."

"What did you tell the police?" Quinn asked, filled with sadness.

"It's an open investigation, a robbery homicide," Park said, lifting a small cup of water from a tray. "I couldn't explain why Frank was there. I had to let them think that he was a burglar in a probable argument with a partner or partners and was killed. Since I am still assigned to the mysterious money that Stanley Cobson had, I said I was doing follow up and I walked into all of this when I reached your house. If I tell my captain that there's a curse, it'll land me in the psych ward."

He watched Quinn with sorrow, he couldn't do anything to ease the pain of losing her child and her husband, just as there was nothing he could do to accept

Piper's death.

"I need to see Dylan and Ashley," Quinn said, struggling with every word.

Park gave her the cup of water. "They are both fine," he said with comfort.

"Riley tried to take Ashley's soul," Quinn struggled to say. "Frank was right, my blood stopped the curse inside her. We'll never know how to stop it inside the carrier. Never."

"Quinn, you're stronger than you know and I promise, you will get through this, in time. All of this is unfair, but for those we loved, their deaths won't be for nothing."

Quinn gulped from the cup and gave it back to him. "We couldn't stop her... the curse is still out there and my little girl is dead."

"I have to go. Ashley called your friend Andi and she has been worried sick about you, she was here but I sent her home. I'll give her a call and let her know you're awake," he said, reaching down to her and kissing her forehead. "I know there's no one alive that can tell me about this same curse that happened a hundred years ago, but there has to be someone out there, that may know this story, that experienced these unexplained suicides, and I'm going to find that person. I don't know how I am going to do it, but I am going to find Ostar and that pen and destroy it, and him. I don't care how far I have to go, I won't stop until it's done."

CHAPTER SIXTEEN

The doll that protected the blood of Ostar surfed the
creek waters until it washed along the shoreline in the
adjacent city. A man picking up trash along the stream
found the doll and stuffed it in his bag. At the end of the
day, the man dumped the trash in a bin that sat at the
entrance of an alley.

That night, an elderly homeless woman began her
routine of digging through the trash with hopes to find
something valuable that she could trade for food or
money. The doll was at the top of the last bag that she
opened. It wasn't anything that appeared to be of value,
but it was interesting enough for her to pull it from the
bag and toss it in her shopping cart.

The woman pushed her cart to a mini mart. She was
harmless and no one seemed to mind when she sat
outside the store, sometimes for hours, asking for change.

Around the corner from the mini mart was what she and others called home.

That night, a van carrying several girls in their late teens drove into the parking lot of the mini mart. The girls were all chatty as they walked past the woman and into the store. Two girls, Sydney and Aubrie, quickly purchased items from the store and were the first to come back out.

"Could you spare some change?" asked the woman.

"Hi, what's your name?" asked Sydney as she began searching her purse for change. She pushed her thick curly black hair out of her face.

"My name is Wanda," she said.

"Well Wanda, you're in luck, I have seven quarters," said Sydney, smiling to the woman as she dropped the coins in her hand.

"Wait here," said Wanda.

Wanda stood, walked to her shopping cart, lifted the doll that she had found and returned to the girls. She handed the doll to Sydney who frowned.

"Oh, that's okay, I'm good," said Sydney, giving a giggle to Aubrie.

As the girls walked towards the van, Sydney glanced back to see that Wanda had become sad and disappointed. She jogged back to her and reached for the doll.

"I'm sorry, it is such a nice doll, I didn't want to take it from you."

"Please, I insist. To repay you for your kindness."

"Thank you," Sydney said, taking the doll and catching up to Aubrie who had already made it back to the van and into her seat.

"You're too kind," Aubrie said with sarcasm. "Maybe we can dump it the next time we stop."

Sydney started playing with the doll.

"It's dirty. Maybe I'll clean it up and keep it. After all, if I can't talk to you during this boring retreat, I'll do my venting to this thing."

They laughed as the other girls and the driver got back in the van.

It was the middle of the night, all of the passengers had fallen asleep except for Sydney and the chaperone who was having quiet conversation with the driver.

Sydney began examining the doll. She flipped it over to see the pocket closed with the tacky adhesive. She opened it and saw the pen.

"Interesting," she whispered.

She removed the pen, placed her foot on the seat and began doodling on the side of her sneaker. Without noticing, the ink from the pen slowly ran down onto her hand, between her finger and her thumb, staining it with the familiar four bars.

Sydney's body briefly jerked. She leaned her head against the window and peered out. Her eyes were blood red from blown vessels and her pupils shimmered as bright as diamonds.